A LOVING PROPOSITION

"I know you have no desire to settle down," Alessia declared. "This is not an attempt to force you into matrimony."

Rhys raised her hand to his lips and kissed it gently. "I know," he said.

"And since I have never met the man who could tempt me to give up my freedom, I doubt I ever will," Alessia went on. "But I see no reason why, simply because I choose never to marry, I should deprive myself of what—every woman has a right to know."

Rhys said nothing. Alessia continued desperately, "I must admit I had . . . expected more help from you. Must I put it in words of one syllable? Although I am unwilling to enter into a matrimonial arrangement with you, I am quite willing—indeed quite anxious—to become your mistress. . . ."

The Talisman

Dawn Lindsey

SIGNET
Published by the Penguin Group
Penguin Books USA Inc., 375 Hudson Street,
New York, New York, U.S.A. 10014
Penguin Books Ltd, 27 Wrights Lane, London W8 5TZ, England
Penguin Books Australia Ltd, Ringwood, Victoria, Australia
Penguin Books Canada Ltd, 2801 John Street, Markham, Ontario,
Canada L3R 1B4
Penguin Books (N.Z.) Ltd, 182-190 Wairau Road,
Auckland 10, New Zealand

Penguin Books Ltd, Registered Offices:
Harmondsworth, Middlesex, England

First published by Signet, an imprint of Penguin Books USA Inc.

First Printing, May, 1990

10 9 8 7 6 5 4 3 2 1

1

The solitary horseman had no premonition of danger. The only trouble he foresaw was another cold day spent in the saddle and the unwelcome leisure to repent his hasty decision to ride north in the tail of a blizzard.

Certainly he had had ample time by then to realize that it had been a mistake to return after so many years. He had left his home in a red-hot rage nearly six years before; and to reappear now as the prodigal—and disinherited—son smacked too nearly of high melodrama for his taste.

His father was dead anyway, which was all that really mattered. Still, stubbornness and a certain ingrained curiosity kept him riding steadily northward, ignoring the growing numbness in his fingers and toes and the icy wind blowing down his neck. He had thought the breach between his father and himself finally healed. To return to England after his death to belatedly discover otherwise in the form of so cold and implacable a will had come as an unpleasant shock.

The worst of the weather had thankfully passed, but the roads were still treacherous underfoot and there was a sharp bite to the east wind that indicated the slush would freeze over again during the night. It also seemed his blood had grown thin from too many years spent in hotter climates, for it seemed to go right through him.

He shrugged under his heavy cloak, knowing he had only himself to blame. His solicitor had warned him to hire a chaise, or at the very least go by post, but he had wanted to take his time and see the countryside again. It served him right for having given in to so uncharacteristically sentimental an impulse.

Not surprisingly, he encountered very little other traffic on the road. Once or twice he overtook a coach making poor headway in the mire, its occupants looking cold and miserable. He was himself beginning to think longingly of a warm fire and a hot meal, for it was an hour past lunch already and breakfast seemed a long time ago.

When he first saw the two riders approaching from the opposite direction he had no other thought than a certain fellow feeling for them. Both were heavily bundled up against the cold and looked as miserable as he felt. His pistol was tucked in his saddlebag out of reach, but it did not occur to him to want it. This was England, after all, not the wilds of Greece or Corsica, where any chance-encountered stranger might be as easily an enemy as a friend, and the wise traveler seldom ventured out alone or unarmed.

He nodded affably as the two approached, anxious to learn from them how near the next village was, and whether it boasted a decent inn or not. Even when one of the horsemen unexpectedly veered across his path and both raised serviceable pistols, it still took him a second to take in the audacity of a holdup in broad daylight.

But a quick glance around showed him that it was not so very audacious after all. On such a day there were few travelers and the road at that point was isolated, hedged in on both sides by a desolate-looking wood. Even though it was barely one o'clock, the sun had already disappeared behind the tops of the leafless trees and it was beginning to grow dark and gloomy.

For that reason he made no attempt to offer any heroic and probably futile resistance. He feared he deserved to lose his watch and purse for being caught so completely off-guard. He therefore pulled to a stop and raised his hands when roughly ordered to, calmly awaiting events.

The man nearer him, his face scarcely visible above a bulky muffler, had quickly dismounted and impatiently gestured him to follow suit. The traveler thought again of the pistol tucked uselessly away in his bags, and did so, glad enough of the chance to stretch his legs. He thankfully stamped his booted feet to try to bring some life back into his frozen toes and stretched painfully cramped muscles.

The man waved him back, brusquely ordering him to empty his pockets in a voice that showed he had a cold starting.

"I warn you I've little enough worth stealing," the traveler said cheerfully enough. "In fact I wouldn't have thought setting on solitary riders a particularly profitable enterprise. But then, I suppose everyone has to eat, and the roads have been pretty thin the last week."

"Shut up!" The man with the cold was plainly in no mood to banter words. In something like disgust, he hefted the slim purse and gold watch produced, and demanded belligerently, "Is that all? No rings or seals?"

"Well, I did warn you I was a most unpromising pigeon. I'll make a deal with you, however. You're welcome to the watch and snuffbox, but leave me my purse, which as you've pointed out is painfully thin but will at least pay for my lodgings for the night. In return I'll undertake not to report you to the nearest magistrate. After all, in this snow your trail will be easy enough to follow."

The man with the cold didn't seem to find this proposal amusing. "Shut up!" he said again. "What's in them saddlebags?"

"Nothing but a change of clothes. I'm used to traveling light. But by all means look for yourself if you don't believe me."

The one on the ground fumbled with the stiff leather straps, swearing a little under his breath. "Nothing but some clothes and a brace o' pops," he growled at last, brandishing the pistol. "Let's get it over and be done with is what I say."

The one on horseback had said nothing, though he had kept his pistol steadily pointed at their victim's heart. "Never mind that," he said now. "Search him."

"What's the point? Someone's likely to diddle us at any minute."

"Just do as you're told. It's got to be on him."

The traveler glanced slowly at him, for the first time beginning to question so unlikely a holdup. But before the suspicion was more than half-formed, something, some instinct of self-preservation, alerted him. He half-turned, throwing up his arm in belated protection even as the deafening report startled a few birds in the wood into raucous flight, and sent the hired nag off down the road at a faster pace than he'd achieved all day.

As the searing pain struck his right arm, then his side, his first inconsequential thought was that he had never stared down the muzzle of a pistol fired at point-blank range before. Funny. They said you never saw the ball that killed you, but it seemed they were mistaken about that, as about so many other things.

His second thought, as he lay in the dirty slush of the road at their feet, had to do with the irony of dying in civilized England after some of the highly uncivilized places he'd been in the last years. It seemed his famous luck had finally run out.

In response to the thought, he instinctively felt for the talisman hanging round his neck, under his clothes, and was reassured to find it still there. But it appeared he had saved the money belt, also hidden around his waist, at the expense of his own life. It was his last coherent thought before the blackness sucked him under completely.

Alessia Fielding, also a most reluctant traveler, found her spirits dropping with every mile her cousin's ponderous traveling coach covered.

She told herself sensibly that it was only natural she should regret the end of so pleasant a holiday. Her friend Theresa, recently married and with a new baby on the way, had been delighted to have her, and had missed no opportunity to make her stay enjoyable. To return to her own humdrum existence after that was bound to be slightly depressing.

It did no good. She knew that she regretted, not the end of her holiday, but the necessity of returning home. And if anyone had told her six months ago that that would be the case, she would have laughed in his face.

Even so, she found herself wishing foolishly that something—anything!—out of the ordinary would happen to prolong the journey. A new fall of snow, a breakdown, even being held up at gunpoint would be a relief, for it would put off the time she must return to Clarissa's unrelenting chatter and her own unworthy jealousy at seeing Cousin Jane queening it over the home that until six months ago had been her own. Even her cousin Henry's simple pride in being Sir Henry Fielding of the Oaks in place of her father had begun to chafe unbearably.

The thought of welcoming a holdup amused her, for she had had ample time in the last six months to discover that hers was not the stuff of which heroines were made. If she had been, she wouldn't now be meekly driving back on a dismal February day to the home that had become little more than a prison to her. She would have had the courage to remove herself and live wherever she chose, in defiance of her relatives' disapproval and society's dictates. She had the means, and Cousin Henry had no real control over her, for she was of legal age.

But that would also mean tearing out her roots and leaving behind everything she held dear, and inviting public censure in a way she cared little to endure. It had been bad enough when she had insisted upon living in the dower house and not under her cousin's roof. And even then she had had to pay the price of agreeing to have a companion live with her in the form of Clarissa Buel, a distant and penniless relative whose annoying ways had quickly begun to drive her to distraction.

The bitter truth was that a good deal of her present gloom was caused by the unwelcome discovery that she was far more craven and conventional than she had ever wanted to believe herself. Which was why she was returning with a heavy heart to a place that until six months ago had been a haven of peace and happiness.

As if aware of her gloomy thoughts, her maid, Potton, glanced at her and observed gruffly, "I daresay it's always sad to leave such an old friend as Mrs. Yardley. But you'll be glad enough to be home once we get there."

Alessia forced a cheerful-enough smile. "Theresa did look blooming, didn't she? And I shall be glad to get out of this weather, at least. It sometimes seems it will never be spring again."

The maid, a tall, unattractive spinster, said no more, and Alessia was grateful for her silence. Had Clarissa been on the journey, she would have had to endure a constant barrage of nonstop chatter, all of it inane and better left unsaid.

Still, she was a little amused that even the thought of being stopped by highwaymen should seem preferable to her at the moment. But then, nothing that exciting was ever likely to happen to her.

It was at that precise point that the heavy traveling coach suddenly came to an abrupt halt, slithering dangerously on the icy road and throwing her forcefully forward onto the opposite seat.

Alessia righted herself, shaken but unharmed, and struck by the aptness of the timing. But since she was an eminently practical woman, despite her recent foolish fantasies, her first thought was not that they were being held up, but that they must have encountered some obstacle on the road.

She had been paying very little attention for miles now, and thought the next village was still some way off, but she looked quickly out of the window now, trying to see what had stopped them. Nothing met her eyes on either side but a frozen wood, and she saw that it had grown later than she had realized. It was almost dusk, and the spot seemed deserted and strangely lonely.

For a moment her careless wish came back again to haunt her; but then she grinned and quickly dismissed it. With two grown men on the box and her maid at her side, she was hardly in any danger;

and had they been held up, James would almost certainly have let off the blunderbuss Henry refused ever to travel without.

At any rate, hadn't she just reluctantly concluded that nothing so adventurous was ever likely to happen to her?

After a moment the door of the coach was pulled open and her footman's cold and apologetic face appeared in the opening. "Beg pardon, Miss Alessia. Are you all right?"

"Perfectly," she answered cheerfully. "Why have we stopped? One of the horses hasn't gone lame, has he?"

"Oh, no, miss." That said, James seemed oddly unwilling to continue, which was unlike him. He scratched his head, hesitated, then at last blurted out, "The truth is, begging your pardon, miss, that there's a body in the road. Horsham and me was wondering what you would want done with it?"

2

It came so pat on her earlier thoughts that for a moment Alessia almost laughed out loud.

Then a glance at James's face, which looked both alarmed and slightly sheepish, sobered her. "Good God," she said blankly. "Are you sure?"

"Oh, yes, miss. There can be no mistake." The footman acted almost as if he were somehow personally responsible for such a solecism. But then, her cousin Henry would undoubtedly frown upon encountering dead bodies on public roads, and would probably indeed hold his servants to blame. It smacked too much of vulgar display.

The thought again amused Alessia briefly, but she bit back the untimely humor. "Good God," she said again. "What do you suggest we do?"

"Aye, that's what me and Horsham were wondering," he acknowledged. "It seemed cruel, like, just to leave it here, but you can hardly take it with you. Horsham thought it best to see what you would wish to be done, Miss Alessia."

She rose with sudden decision and prepared to descend. "Of course we can't just leave it here. Where is it?"

She emerged, a tall slender figure in her somber black traveling dress, her hat and pelisse trimmed with sables that were no richer than her midnight hair and equally dark eyes, her booted feet crunching on the now-refreezing snow.

The coachman was a little way up the road, bending over an ominous bundle. He straightened at the sound of her approach and warned hastily, "Best stay back, Miss Alessia! It's not a sight for a lady's eyes."

"Nonsense. What did he die of? Do you know?"

The body was lying on its face in the dirty slush, its arms outstretched. It was nearly dusk, so that for a moment it looked as if he had simply collapsed there.

Then she saw the blood.

There was a great quantity of it staining the dirty snow and stretching in a dreadful path behind him into the woods. It seemed obvious he had been wounded somewhere in the woods, and somehow managed to reach the road before collapsing and dying.

The thought was somehow horrible, and she swallowed, for a moment wishing she had obeyed her coachman's warning. Visions of poachers, or animal traps in the wood beyond, and a man left to die in the snow as indicated by that dreadful trail of blood conjured up far too vivid a series of mental pictures for her comfort.

Horsham gingerly turned the body over. "Shot, he reported grimly.

"*Shot*?" Shock managed to dispel her brief dizziness. "Are you sure?"

"Yes, miss. Must've been robbers, though I've never known them to kill their victim—at least in these parts."

"Good God, no! What would be the point? At any rate, I've never even heard of anyone being held up around here."

"No, miss. But then, there's always a first time," the coachman pointed out practically. "And his pockets have been turned out, all right. Must've been robbery."

She could not prevent another unwilling look

downward. The body was now lying on its back in the deepening gloom. His clothes were so wet and stained it was impossible to tell their quality, though she saw with a shudder that he was both young and would not have been ill-favored under other circumstances. He lay in the dirty slush of the road, one arm pulled across as he was turned over and now partly shadowing his face. Only the hand, surprisingly well-kept, gave any clue to his class. It lay with the fingers curled up, looking as if they had been carved from marble.

She shivered, suddenly feeling the piercing wind. The crimson stain at his breast seemed to tell its own tale, and her earlier foolish desire for a delay of any kind came back to haunt her. She could scarcely contemplate taking such a hideous thing up with her, but nor could she simply leave it there.

"W-wrap him—it—up as best you can, and we'll take it to the next village," she pronounced unwillingly. "It's the least we can do."

Despite her resolve, she glanced again at the body as Horsham prepared to do her bidding. Another deep shudder took her, and she was about to turn quickly away when something stopped her.

For a moment she didn't know what it was. Then a faint movement, the merest flicker in that marble-like hand, drew a strangled cry of horror from her.

It was only for a brief moment that the hour and the eerie circumstances had her thinking the unthinkable. The next instant she was on her knees by the body. "He's not dead yet!" she cried frantically. "I saw him move! Quick, get me the brandy and something warm to wrap him with. He's half-frozen. In fact it's a miracle he's still alive, for there's no telling how long he's been lying out here."

When she felt for it, she could detect the faintest hint of a pulse in his neck, though his flesh was icy to her touch. She glanced around quickly for the brandy, only to find both of her henchmen staring at her as if stupefied.

"Good God, don't just stand there! Hurry! Every moment could be vital!"

James at last reluctantly went back to the coach, but luckily Potton had emerged by then, wasting no precious time on useless questions.

Alessia gratefully accepted the brandy flask from her and tried to get some of it down the man's throat, while Potton efficiently tucked the carriage rug around him. They were both kneeling in the slush of the road, soaking their skirts, but neither bothered to notice.

Most of the brandy trickled uselessly out of his mouth again, but Alessia had seen another flicker of that hand, and said urgently, "We must get him warm and dry! He's alive, but only just, and I imagine the cold is as much a danger as his wound."

At her sharp order, James and Horsham reluctantly lifted his long limp body and conveyed it awkwardly to the coach. "Though if you was to ask me, he's three-parts dead already," James pronounced pessimistically.

Alessia was surprised at how instinctively she recoiled from the probable truth of his words. "Don't say that!" she cried furiously. "Lift him carefully. I'll take his head in my lap to steady him."

Again her henchmen hesitated. "Beg pardon, Miss Alessia," protested Horsham apologetically, "but you'll ruin your fur."

"Oh, what does it matter, you fool? Hurry. For God's sake, hurry."

They finally did as she asked, lifting their lifeless burden onto the seat beside her. He was dreadfully wet, and she shivered a little despite herself at her unpleasant burden, but ordered quickly, "Now drive as fast as possible to the nearest house. A hovel will do! We've got to get him warm."

The two servants exchanged wary looks. "Aye, me and Horsham was discussing that just now," James admitted. "There's a small village not too far from here, but it's little more than a few cottages and an inn catering to the locals. There ain't likely to be a doctor within thirty miles or more," he warned.

"If there's an inn, then go there! We'll worry about a doctor later. My first concern is getting him warm and dry, or he almost certainly will die."

Still they hesitated, so that she was ready to scream in frustration. "Beg pardon, Miss Alessia," Horsham said now, even more unwillingly, "but have you forgotten Sir Henry will be expecting you tonight?"

She closed her eyes for a long moment, thinking she had stumbled into a nightmare from which there seemed no awakening. "Never mind that. Even Sir Henry can scarcely expect me to leave a man to die upon the road. Now, get us to that inn and don't hesitate to spring 'em!"

Horsham still hesitated, plainly unhappily remembering his employer's strict prohibition against anything more rackety than a sedate trot. But finally he seemed to think better of it and shrugged, and at last went to climb back up onto the box.

Whether or not he was glad for an excuse to break his rigid instructions or whether the sense of urgency had gotten through to him at last, Alessia was relieved to see that the coachman took her at her literal word. After the plodding pace of the earlier part of the journey, the sudden speed was all the more welcome.

But she was soon to regret her rash words, for she had her hands full keeping her unconscious passenger on the seat and sheltering him from the worst jolts of the road.

He had shown no more signs of consciousness, but in the failing light she thought that his color had improved slightly. Once again she tried to force some brandy down his throat, but in the swaying vehicle it was largely a futile effort. In the end she had to content herself with keeping the rug tucked around him and cradling his wet head in her lap.

From what she could see of him, he had an interesting-enough face. He was not precisely handsome by the definition of the day, which favored Byronic languor, but there was something about the strong planes of his cheeks and the set of his mouth that was arresting.

His hair was overlong and shaggy, and at present artificially dark from the moisture, but it looked as though it would be an unremarkable straw color naturally. His complexion, though waxlike at the moment, was unfashionably brown, as if he had spent much time outdoors or been living in a warmer climate.

She could see little more of him, but that his nose was aggressive and surprisingly straight, his brows fair, and his mouth well-molded. An intriguing crease ran from nose to mouth in the lean cheek nearer her, seeming to indicate he was more accustomed to laughing than frowning.

Certainly, from the length of him in the restricted coach, he was taller than average, though he was by no means stockily built. His head lay heavily against her thighs, however, the dampness beginning to seep unpleasantly through her skirts.

It seemed to her, perhaps fancifully, that he had been a vital, attractive man. Certainly he was far too young to die so lonely and dreadful a death in the snow.

Even so, she knew realistically that it would be folly to allow herself to become too involved with this stranger. Despite her intervention, he was very near death, and every second's delay in getting help to him was likely to prove fatal. He must possess a will of iron to have dragged himself onto the road and survived as long as he had.

Nor had she any way of knowing how long he'd lain there, or how much blood might have been lost. But the combination of loss of blood and extreme cold was depressingly likely to prove fatal even if his wound did not.

She couldn't help wondering in horror who could have shot him and left him for dead in the snow. She knew little of robbers, of course, but it seemed unlikely they would bother to murder their victims.

But that left her with even more unpalatable options. If not a simple robbery, the other reason she could think of for someone shooting him and leaving him for dead in the snow were even more horrible. A falling-out among thieves. A private feud. A quarrel over a woman. Almost anything might be possible.

She knew she was allowing her imagination to run away with her and tried to quell such disturbing thoughts. But the memory of that long trail of blood into the woods continued to haunt her.

Worse, James was right. The chances were high that he would die without ever regaining consciousness, despite her efforts. Even if by some miracle he did not, she was unlikely ever to see him again after tonight. She would turn him over to someone in authority in the next village and resume her journey, with nothing left to remind her of the night's unexpected adventure but a ruined traveling dress and Jane's disapproval. She was a fool to allow herself to become emotionally involved, and the sooner she got home and stopped her foolishness, the better.

It was then, again as if in defiance of her thoughts, that the head on her lap stirred. Alessia jumped, and found herself staring down into a pair of surprisingly light amber-colored eyes.

For a moment there was nothing but a puzzled vagueness in them. Then he blinked, and seemed to pull himself up with an effort, for they took on a semblance of awareness.

He stared at her for a moment longer, a faint frown between his fair brows, as if trying to make sense of his surroundings. Then he remarked clearly, "I must still be dreaming. Either that or fate is playing one last trick on me. I've never believed in an afterlife, and I certainly never thought that heaven would be my final destination. But how else to explain waking to find myself in the arms of an angel?"

Even on the words his eyes drifted closed, and he lost consciousness once more.

3

Fate, however, seemed to be intent on repaying Alessia in full for her earlier folly, for she found she was unable to wash her hands of her unknown passenger in the next village.

It was little more than a huddle of cottages, as her coachman had predicted, and the landlord at the only modest inn showed absolutely no inclination to burden himself with a wounded traveler whose pockets had been emptied of all money and identification, and who was likely to die on him before he could contact any relatives.

As he pointed out, even if he had had the inclination to take on so thankless a task, he had no time to be tending to an invalid. His wife had been dead some eighteen months and he ran the inn alone. And since his was the only taproom for miles, he had little spare time at all, let lone to be running up and down the stairs fetching hot broth and changing bandages.

When Alessia suggested that someone might be hired in the village to do so, he assured her it was the same for everyone else. They had no time to be nursing strangers and no desire to take on such a responsibility. He could only recommend that she drive on to the nearest town and turn her patient over to the proper authorities. The local magistrate was the one she should be addressing, not an overworked innkeeper.

Alessia came very close to losing her temper in the face of such callousness. Only the sudden unwelcome realization that she, too, had been trying to rid herself of so inconvenient a passenger kept the hot words about Christian duty and common charity guiltily unspoken.

It was then she found herself uncomfortably face-to-face with her own conscience. She had just been longing for something out of the ordinary to happen. But now that it had, and she was caught up, willy-nilly, in a genuine adventure, she, like the landlord, could think only of her own convenience. Clarissa would be expecting her, and Jane and Henry shocked at her involvement in so potentially scandalous a situation. At any rate, any well-bred lady would naturally shrink from taking on the nursing of a total stranger, let alone putting up at an inferior inn with no more than a maid for chaperone. The situation was rife with potential awkwardness and impropriety. It was, in fact, unthinkable.

Except that he would obviously die without immediate help. And she had the sinking feeling that if she turned her back on this heaven-sent opportunity, so unexpectedly offered, to escape her tedious life even for a short while, she deserved every dreary moment that was undoubtedly coming to her. She had longed for the courage to run away, but it required very little courage to remain and do what any halfway compassionate person would do. She had only to write to Clarissa that she was remaining a little longer with her friend, and the thing was done. It would never occur to anyone to ask awkward questions, and with any luck, no one need ever know anything about it.

And if she did not—if she gave in to convention and convenience and let a man die because of it—then she would be faced with admitting, finally and irrevocably, that she was as spineless and weak-willied as she had come to think herself lately.

She lifted her head, aware of the three servants' worried expressions and the landlord's impatience. "Very well," she said, her chin coming up a little in defiance. "I will stay and nurse him myself, then. I will require the hire of your entire house, except for the taproom, of course, and what assistance you can give me. It may be necessary to hire another maid in the village, but if so, I will naturally pay for it. As soon as we have the patient comfortable, James may ride for the doctor, if you will give him directions, and Horsham can take a note to my family."

She was surprised at how immediately free the decision made her, and after that, ignored all objections. She had the patient carried up to the best bedchamber, allowed Horsham and James to strip him and ensconce him in the large bed, then with Potton undertook the gory task of cleaning his wound.

That, at least, nearly succeeded in shaking her newfound resolve. She discovered he had evidently tried to protect himself at the last minute, for the ball not only entered his left breast, just below his heart, but also plowed through the muscle of his right upper arm first. It was that that had undoubtedly saved him, for the ball must have lost a good deal of its velocity. It had also been further deflected by his ribs, but even so, both wounds were far worse than she had imagined. She feared a little sickly that if she had seen them earlier she might not have been so brave after all, for she had almost no experience of such wounds.

The weather had probably helped as well, for though he had undoubtedly lost a lot of blood in his struggles to reach the road, the extreme cold had slowed the bleeding. Both wounds were only seeping sluggishly now.

The landlord had unwillingly sent up a quantity of lint and hot water, and so Alessia gingerly cleaned the wounds as best she could, then dared do no more than bandage them loosely against the doctor's coming. Her patient had not stirred again, but in the lanternlight, and with his face cleaned and his hair dried, proved surprisingly presentable.

The doctor, when he at last came, seemed, like the landlord, to resent the claims of an unknown traveler likely to die anyway before the night was out. He grudgingly consented to remove the ball still lodged in the patient's chest, diagnosed and strapped up a couple of broken ribs, and predicted bluntly that the patient wouldn't live to see the morning. If the loss of blood didn't kill him, very likely pneumonia would, for he was dangerously chilled. It was a miracle he had survived so long already.

Alessia was surprised at how she bristled at his pessimism, and was not sorry when he declined to come again unless specifically sent for.

Nevertheless his words remained a cold lump in her throat, and she spent the first night in a chair by her patient's bedside, dreading at any minute to discover that even the shallow rise and fall of his chest, under the uncomfortable-looking bandages, had ceased.

But contrary to all predictions, he didn't die that first night. By morning, however, he was suffering from deep chills, and it was all she and Potton both could do to keep him warm. His body shook with ague, but he fought being covered as if it represented some horror to him, and even as ill as he was, he was surprisingly strong. Alessia was in constant dread that he would tear his wounds open and start the bleeding all over again.

Thankfully, by evening the chills had gone, to be replaced by a raging fever. For the next two days he was delirious, often crying out unintelligently and scrabbling at his throat, as if searching for something.

But still he did not die. Alessia herself was exhausted by then, but she had little time to regret or even reflect on the decision she had made.

Potton had proved a capable, unflappable nurse, though she made little attempt to hide her misgivings. James, too, was invaluable in helping to turn the patient and holding him while they changed his dressings, though he obviously disapproved of Alessia's actions. Like Horsham, however, he had been in her father's employ long before Cousin Henry's, and so would have died rather than betray her.

For herself, despite everything, Alessia was continually amazed at how free she felt. Getting very little sleep, tending to an extremely ill man whose identity she didn't know and who seldom spoke, and then only in delirium, could hardly be considered riotous living. The weather continued inclement as well, which meant that she was more or less tied by her heels indoors. She often took a late walk in the evenings, but the raw wind and uninspiring scenery invariably soon drove her inside again. In addition, the accommodations were primitive, the companionship extremely limited, and her means for amusing herself during the long hours reduced to mending her patient's clothes, cleaned and returned to a modicum of respectability, and reading the one book she had brought with her.

But none of that seemed to matter. She felt

needed and useful, and not even the enforced intimacies of the sickroom overly bothered her. She sponged her patient dispassionately, helped to change his dressings, and thought nothing of lifting his head to turn his pillows or smooth his tumbled sheets.

But she knew that in truth she was far from being in the least dispassionate about him. With nothing else to occupy her thoughts, she speculated endlessly about him as she sat quietly reading or sewing by the fire. Certainly he had long since ceased to be a stranger whose death she would regret but not mourn.

But she was also wise enough to realize that that was likely to prove a dangerous indulgence. Even if her patient didn't die, as she was finally beginning to hope, she knew nothing about him. Her vivid imagination might have invented a hundred possible reasons for his having been shot and left to die in the snow, but despite his noble profile, he was every bit as likely to prove a thief himself, or wanted for some dreadful crime, instead of the romantic hero of the wilder of her imaginations.

At any rate, she hoped she had not yet reached the state in which she must eke out her dreary life by imagining intrigue where none existed, and romance out of whole cloth. Very likely her patient was merely some unremarkable man caught up in remarkable events, just as she was, and probably had a wife and five children somewhere.

If so, there was nothing to hint of either among his clothes or few possessions. They had found, when James undressed him, a money belt hidden under his clothes, containing a fairly substantial amount, which at least spoke of some substance. But what he was doing on the road at all, or if he had been accompanied, as seemed probable—and if so, what had happened to his companions—remained a mystery.

The only possible clue to his identity lay in a curiously carved ring he had worn on a chain around his neck, but it bore no engraving or initials or a recognizable coat of arms. Aside from that, there had been no visiting cards in his pockets, not even so much as a letter or piece of paper that might help identify him. It was not hard to conclude that whoever had shot him had not intended that his identity should ever be discovered.

Which argued that he was not from that district, or someone would surely have reported him missing long since. His clothes, too, seemed to be subtly different, as if they had not been made in England. Nor could she forget his unfashionable darkness, as if he had spent much time in hotter climates, though it was already beginning to fade now.

His chest and arms were also unnaturally brown above the deep white of the bandages, and were surprisingly muscular, as if he were used to manual labor. But his hands were well-kept, and his voice, even in delirium, obviously cultured.

All in all, he was a most annoying puzzle. She sometimes thought she was determined to keep him alive only to satisfy her own curiosity about him.

She was speculating about him one night, almost a week after they had first arrived, and had forgotten her embroidery to sit, her chin propped in her hands, her straight brows knit in a frown as she watched him. She had forgotten the passing time or the rest of the house, long since retired for the night. The only sounds to disturb her were the occasional creak of a board as the house settled, and the quiet crackling of the fire.

She didn't know when she first became aware

that something was different about the silence. She came out of her trance to find that her patient's head had turned toward her on the pillow and his eyes were open and resting on her.

Her heart stirred unaccountably, and she rose quickly and went to his bedside, automatically putting a hand to his brow. For once it seemed fairly cool.

At her touch he murmured weakly, as if in satisfaction, "My angel. I was beginning to fear I'd only dreamed you."

She couldn't help laughing. "You're very far from being dead, and no one has ever accused me of being an angel before. How are you feeling?"

"Like I've been trampled by a herd of elephants," he complained, stirring weakly. "*Am* I dreaming?"

"No, your fever seems to be down, though you have been very ill. But since there are no elephants in England, I doubt that's what happened to you. Would you like something to drink? I have some lemonade here."

He seemed content to let her raise his head, and sipped gratefully at the glass she held to his lips. But even that brief effort seemed to exhaust him. When she laid him back down again, he closed his eyes wearily.

She started to tiptoe away, but surprisingly he stopped her. "No, don't go," he murmured. "I'm not asleep. And I'm afraid you'll disappear again. May I at least know your name? Or don't angels have names?"

"It's Alessia," she said, as if to a child. "But don't try to talk anymore."

"Alessia," he repeated, testing it. "Am I in Italy, then? I thought I must have dreamed that as well."

"Hush. We'll talk about it later. Go back to sleep now," she said soothingly.

Instead he raised a hand to his throat, as she had seen him do a number of times, as if he were searching for something. She hesitated, then went to fetch the ring on a chain that she had removed for safekeeping that first night, and put it into his left hand.

His fingers closed gratefully around it and he sighed. "Ah, they didn't get it, then. I feared—"

"No, they didn't get it. Go to sleep now. You're safe with me."

Even as she said it, she felt foolish, but he seemed to accept it and obediently closed his eyes again. This time she waited until she thought he was alseep before trying to withdraw.

Instantly his left hand came out weakly to grasp her wrist. "Don't go," he said again, his hand tightening. "Promise me you won't leave me, Angel."

She hesitated for only a moment, then answered softly, "No, I won't leave you."

Even to her ears it sounded oddly like a vow.

4

The next time the patient opened his eyes, he was no longer tempted to believe he was dead. There was too much pain for that.

He tried to be grateful for the fact, but found it beyond him at the moment. Every breath he drew was an agony, and his body felt like an alien thing that had turned against him. There was a fire in his head, and another in his chest, and one arm seemed strapped down and useless to him. He began to long again for the half-dead drifting state he had been in for so long and which had been far more pleasant.

Immediately he looked around for his angel, but her chair by the fireside was empty. He suffered a pang, again half-afraid he had only imagined her. But she—or at least someone—had been there very recently, for the fire was made up, the room tidy, and his covers smooth.

At least his mind was clearer now. To distract it from his almost overwhelming physical ills, he gradually tried to piece together the vague fragments of memory dancing around in his head.

He had been riding. That much he remembered, though he couldn't immediately remember where he was or where he had been going. Had he been shot? He seemed to remember staring down the barrel of a pistol, thinking incredulously that he could see death streaking toward him.

But it seemed he hadn't died after all. He could only think he must still be in Greece, and had been wounded in battle, although "battle" was too dignified a name for those badly planned, ill-equipped skirmishes in which fanaticism was expected to make up for the lack of arms, and neither side knew the meaning of compromise. He had been a fool to allow himself to get caught up in it.

And if he were still in Greece, why then did he have so distinct a memory of cold, and his face half-buried in snow? He knew the mind could play remarkable tricks on one, but he could still remember the grainy texture of it, and the numbing sting against his face, as well as the creeping chill as the damp gradually soaked through his clothes all the way to his bones.

And where did his angel fit into it all?

Snow. England. Yes, he was beginning to remember now. But how did he come to be wounded, if not in a battle?

Ah. He had been held up. It was slowly coming back to him. There had been two of them. He had been foolishly caught off-guard, and they had taken his purse and then been angry with the little he was carrying. He remembered joking with them about the unprofitability of their enterprise.

It would appear to have been an ill-timed jest. They seemed to have been annoyed enough to shoot him and leave him for dead as a consequence. He wondered if they had found his hidden belt, but not enough to care one way or the other.

Certainly he remembered his own disbelief as he stared into the muzzle of the pistol and his far-too-belated attempt to escape. Then nothing more for some time. They had obviously moved him off the road, for he had awakened in a dark wood, the naked branches towering far above his head and the ice beneath his cheek still frozen in the deep shade.

At first he had been relieved that they had not bothered to finish him off. But soon enough had come the unwelcome realization that the cold and shock from loss of blood were likely to do their dirty work for them.

He had had no idea in which direction the road lay, or how far he might be from civilization, but he remembered too drearily well how little traffic there had been out on such a day. It was far too late to regret not having listened to Kettlewell's warning; but for a long while he had had to resist the overwhelming desire just to close his eyes and drift off again, leaving the future to settle itself.

Ah, Kettlewell. He was beginning to remember at last. His father's death and his own belated return to England. Then that odd business about the will and his impulsive decision to go to Crickfield himself. Well, Kettlewell had warned him, though undoubtedly he had only discomfort and inconvenience in mind. Being shot and left for dead by highwaymen was far outside the solicitor's limited imagination.

But it had happened, and to die in the snow in England would have been ironic, to put it mildly.

He had seen the effects of extreme cold before, and had known by the degree of his lassitude and the fact he no longer felt the cold at all that he would die quickly if he didn't get help soon.

But then, he knew it was very likely he would die anyway, for he felt disastrously sick and disoriented. It was only some small comfort that he felt very little pain. Even when he made himself move at last, clumsily and with little control over his limbs, he felt no protest.

He was sweating and panting with exertion by the time he had managed to pull himself up to a sitting position, despite the rapidly dropping temperature.

His right arm was almost useless, but he examined what he could see of his wounds and concluded in relief that neither was immediately fatal, nor even bleeding very much now. The snow around him betrayed the amount of blood he'd lost, but apparently his ribs had deflected the ball from doing more serious damage.

Obviously his instinctive turn at the end, when facing the truth of a cocked pistol aimed straight at his heart, had saved his life. But then, he had always had the devil's own luck.

Ironically, even the cold had helped, though it threatened now to reverse the favor. He had no idea how long he had been unconscious, though the lengthening shadows attested to some time. But he would almost certainly have bled to death long since if the cold hadn't slowed the bleeding.

Even so, he was light-headed and uncoordinated when he at last succeeded in getting to his feet. He reeled from tree to tree like a drunken man, and again blessed the cold for numbing almost all feeling. Even his good arm and legs didn't want to do his bidding, but he still felt no active pain. Only a growing sense of numbness and extreme unreality, as if it couldn't be happening to him.

He still had no idea in which direction the road lay, but since he was in highly populated England, not the wilds of Greece as he had first feared, he had hopes that in almost any direction he went he would soon enough find some signs of habitation. And by dint of his phenomenal luck, he had in the end stumbled onto a road, though he had no idea if it was the same one he had been traveling on.

He was by that time so spent that when the trees at last ran out, he had had to crawl and drag himself the last painful yards. And as he lay there, sick and exhausted in the snow, he had realized that at dusk on a frozen evening it was likely to prove a wasted effort. It might be morning before there was any more traffic, and he would surely be long dead before then.

For the first time since he had regained consciousness, he began to seriously face the unpalatable likelihood that he was going to die at the side of a well-kept road in civilized England, after all the dangerous and highly uncivilized places he had been in the last six years.

But on the principle of staking everything on the last throw, he had dragged himself out to the middle of the road and collapsed there. He would likely either be run over in the dark or die of exposure, but at least he would be discovered sooner or later.

And it was only then, as he lay facedown in the frozen road, that he had remembered the most extraordinary part of the afternoon's events. Nor could he be certain he hadn't imagined the odd words, for there was little doubt he had been prey to distracting hallucinations ever since. For a while, as he lay in the road, he had imagined himself back on a beach in Italy, hearing the surf pound and feeling the warmth of the hot sun soak into him.

He had clung to the miraculous image of warmth; but the next time he'd regained consciousness it was back in the cold again, to find himself being roughly lifted and carried some distance. That had seemed no more real to him than the earlier dreams had been. He heard a worried voice saying, "Careful, Miss Alessia!" and had been unsurprised. Alessia. An Italian name. He was in Italy, then.

But for some reason they were speaking English, for the voice was going on, very near to his head, "It seems a shame to ruin your furs, miss, for he's bleeding like a stuck pig."

Then a cool, musical voice had answered impatiently, "Never mind that! Just be careful not to jar him."

He had been lowered to a soft surface, and something warm and wonderfully comforting was tucked around him. For a moment he, too, had spared an absurd thought for the fur he was undoubtedly bleeding all over, and regretted its ruin.

He should undoubtedly have protested, but instead snuggled his cheek into it gratefully, aware that this was only a dream as well. The pillow beneath his head seemed surprisingly warm and vital, but he was beyond voicing his gratitude.

Later still he had roused, or dreamed he had, and looked straight up into a beautiful face and soft dark eyes, and known for certain he was dead. It had struck him forcibly that if this was indeed death, there had been no point in struggling so hard. Nothing could be more desirable.

But it seemed he was not dead, and when next he'd opened his eyes the angel had turned into a disapproving spinsterish figure very much like his father's old housekeeper. He could almost regret his return to life. He should have known there'd be no such pleasant afterlife for him.

He turned his head carefully on his pillow now to search again for his angel, or even the dour figure who had supplanted her, but the room was still stubbornly empty. He had no idea where he was, or who had rescued him. It was obviously nighttime. But which night, and how long he had been unconscious, he had no way of knowing.

Then he heard a faint rustle, and felt a cool soft hand on his fevered brow. The voice he had heard once before in his dreams said gently, "So you're awake again. Good. How are you feeling now?"

He minutely adjusted his head, fearful of adding

to his discomfort, and was at last rewarded with a renewed vision of his angel. She was all in black, which struck him as vaguely disturbing; but it little mattered at the moment. The firelight turned her dark hair to a fiery halo around her head, and her face was as gentle and beautiful as he'd remembered it. She had liquid dark eyes, filled with concern, and dark straight brows, and an exquisitely tender mouth. The rest of her disappeared into the shadows, so that her face was all he could see, but it was enough for now.

She raised his head and gave him some more of the cool liquid to drink. Again he was content to be waited on, and sipped gratefully, pleasingly enveloped by her scent and beauty.

"Alessia," he murmured, and closed his eyes and drifted off to sleep once more.

5

When next he woke, he was amazed at how much stronger he felt. Unconsciously he turned his head, to be rewarded by the sight of his angel sitting quietly by the fire, sewing.

She looked up then, as if instantly aware of his glance on her, and rose quickly to cross to him. She placed her soft, cool hand on his forehead, and he thought that never had anything felt so wonderful.

When she would have pulled her hand away again he reached up weakly to catch it. "I'm not feverish anymore," he protested. "I even remember you. You're my angel and you have gentle hands and tender eyes. Even in my delirium you were the one thing I clung to."

She seemed amused by the notion, but made no attempt to draw her hand away. "You've still a touch of fever," she cautioned. "But since it's a miracle you're alive at all, even that's a considerable improvement. How are you feeling tonight?"

"Weak as the devil. And also betrayed. I seem to remember you promised to stay with me. But several times I've awakened to find, not an angel at my bedside, but a disapproving gorgon."

She gave a silvery laugh that enchanted him, as everything about her did. "That's my maid, Potton. But you do her an injustice. She's no gorgon, I promise you."

"Yes, but she obviously doesn't approve of me," he complained. "And she hasn't your gentle touch."

"Never mind. It's me she disapproved of, not you. Are you thirsty?"

"I feel as if I could drink the entire Mediterranean."

She again gently lifted his head to help him drink. "Not all at one time, I hope. The doctor warned me you shouldn't have too much at once."

He drank thirstily, then grimaced and laid his head back on the pillow, his eyes closing weakly. "Thank you. I must be in worse shape than I thought, for I seem to be as weak as a cat. And though I'm grateful for your kindness, I'm sorry to say I've improved enough so that other considerations have begun to intrude. In fact I'm an ungrateful wretch, for you shouldn't be waiting on me hand and foot. Beyond every other consideration, I must look like the very devil."

She laughed and stood back to consider him. "You have a week's growth of beard and you're understandably weak," she remarked gravely. "But you must be improving if you're starting to think of your appearance. And they say women are the ones who are vain."

He felt his rough jaw. "I shall have to shave."

"I would suggest you take one thing at a time. Which reminds me, that's the second time you've made a reference to an exotic locale. The last time you woke, you complained of feeling as if you'd been trampled by a herd of elephants."

"Then I've improved. Now I only feel as if I'd had a family of baboons dancing over my ribs."

"A vast improvement, no doubt!" she agreed in amusement. "But then, you barely escaped a bullet through your heart, and a couple of your ribs seem to have gotten in its way. You also lost a good deal of blood, so it's no wonder you're weak and sore."

"Yes, but I've always been phenomenally lucky." He was enjoying watching the firelight play over her expressive face, and gave up the exhausting struggle to make any sense of it all. "As witness the fact that I'm shot and left for dead, and wake up to find myself being nursed by a beautiful and mysterious woman. Did you know you have an enchanting laugh, by the way?"

She seemed unmoved by the compliment. "Good heavens! Why mysterious? I assure you I'm the most ordinary of creatures."

"Because I seem to see you only at night. It is night now, isn't it? In fact I'm beginning to wonder if you aren't just some fabrication of my fevered brain after all."

"It *is* night. But the answer is far more prosaic, I fear. Once your fever broke, my maid and I have taken it in turn to sit with you. She sleeps during the night and I the day, though hers is by far the more arduous duty, I assure you. At night you've done little more than sleep so far."

"Then I shall have to take care to remedy that," he countered promptly.

She had finished smoothing his sheets and now deftly turned his pillow for him. "I can see you were far less trouble when you were delirious. There. Is that better?"

"Mmm. Much. You clearly *are* an angle, whatever you say," he murmured, content to close his eyes once more.

But when she would have slipped away again, he opened them to complain, "Why are you always running away?"

"I'm not running away. I'll be right here. But you've done enough talking for one night."

"I can't sleep so long as so many questions are

whirling around in my head. And I am resolved to sleep only in the daytime now—to avoid the gorgon, of course."

She gave her delicious laugh again. "Of course! Very well. What do you want to know?"

"First and most important, *is* your name Alessia?"

Her straight dark brows came together in surprise. "Yes, but why on earth should that be most important?"

"Ah, then I didn't dream it," he said in satisfaction.

"No, but surely you have more pressing questions than that?"

"Other questions, but none more pressing. I was dreaming for a while that I was back in Italy, you see, and you were a part of it. I'm relieved to see it wasn't all part of my fantasies."

"And I am beginning to see you are a practiced flirt," she told him severely, obviously trying not to laugh.

He looked wounded. "Where I've been, there were precious few women to practice on, believe me, and none worthy of the effort. Most were wrapped to the eyes and smelled of dirty goats."

"Trying, I'll admit. But that's yet another mysterious reference. I already suspected that you hadn't spent this miserable winter in England. Have you just come from Italy, then?"

"I thought I was supposed to be asking the questions?"

She folded her hands demurely in her lap, her eyes twinkling, and dutifully waited. "Very well, then. The sooner you finish, the sooner you can get some rest. I only hope the next will prove more important than the first."

"Much more important. Why are you in black?

I thought at first I was back in the Mediterranean. Either that or I'd stumbled on my own funeral. But you are obviously far too kindhearted to be quite so tactless. At any rate, black doesn't become you," he added plaintively, considering the matter. "With your coloring you should be in crimson and old gold and emerald. I've seen enough women decked out in funereal black to last me a lifetime."

"I am sure my coloring is little different from the women you so much despised who smelled of goats," she countered. "And I can see you are still plainly out of your head from the fever. Crimson indeed! But if you must know, my father died six months ago. Does that satisfy you?"

"No, but I suppose I must be content for the moment. I feared you were a widow, which would have been disappointing, though certainly not an insurmountable obstacle."

Her eyes widened, and then she said severely, "It has become more than apparent to me what you were doing abroad. Clearly you are a dangerous lunatic. And that's enough questions for now. You've wasted too much energy on nonsense for one night."

"Not nonsense. I like the way your mouth prims up when you're trying not to laugh, by the way," he murmured. "And I'll agree to go to sleep only on one condition: that you'll be here when I wake up again. You promised not to leave me, remember."

"Things were *much* better when you were still delirious," she said severely. "But I'm not going anywhere."

He closed his eyes in satisfaction and drifted off to sleep.

True to his word, he seemed to make it a point the next day to sleep during the daylight hours.

Potton reported to Alessia that he was making a surprisingly rapid recovery, and added darkly that it was a good thing. He was both impudent and likely soon to prove an impossible patient, and the sooner they were rid of him, the better.

Alessia was by no means so ready to agree. Once he was fully recovered, she would have no excuse for lingering any longer, and she had discovered she was oddly content. She had feared the inevitable awkwardness once her patient became conscious, but he was so outrageous, and so amusing, that it was impossible for her to feel any constraint with him.

But for all her speculation about him, she discovered she had never quite managed to put a personality to the face she had come to know so well. Now, in a few short minutes, he had somehow banished all her absurd imaginings, and stamped himself so irrevocably on her consciousness that it was strange to think they had exchanged only a very few words, after all.

Indeed, she was a little amazed at the bond that had grown up between them. He seemed to know instinctively when she was in the room, and she always recognized the moment when his eyes opened and his head turned toward her in the firelight.

He did that now, evidently pleased by her almost instant response to him. "Ah," he said in satisfaction as she rose and crossed the room to his side, "I was dreaming about you just now."

She saw that he looked even stronger than he had the night before. His eyes were clearer and his smile quite definitely more potent. "None of your flattery tonight," she told him severely. "Potton says you are impudent, and I very much fear she's right. How are you feeling? Still like a family of baboons?"

He looked pained. "Not like a family of baboons," he protested. "As if a family of baboons had been *dancing* on my ribs. And I am still undoubtedly delirous, for you seem to grow more beautiful every time I see you. Come and cool my fevered brow."

She laughed, but obligingly put her hand on his warm brow. "Your fever is down again. Dr. Claypole will be amazed, for he objected strongly to being hauled out on a freezing night to save you, and predicted you would never survive. But then, Potton says you have the constitution of an ox."

"Unflattering, but probably true. She still obviously disapproves of me. Were you the one who found me, then?"

" 'Stumbled over you' would be nearer the truth. I nearly ran over you with my coach."

"You see how lucky I am. But however worthy, Potton is wrong about one thing. *You're* the reason I've made such an amazing recovery. I told you the vision of you is the only thing that kept me clinging to life."

"And I'm surprised Italy was far enough away to be safe for you!" she pronounced in disapproval. "Irate fathers and husbands could very easily have reached you there. It's a miracle one of them hasn't long since murder—"

Then, as she realized what she'd said, she broke off in some confusion. "Oh, Lord! I didn't mean . . . *Was* that what . . . ? No! I shouldn't ask."

He eyed her obvious confusion in some amusement, and grinned. "Not to the best of my knowledge. And do you know, I think you're the most remarkable girl I've ever met."

She blushed and was annoyed at so missish a gesture. "If you mean I let my wretched tongue betray me into saying highly unbecoming things, I must agree with you. But you seem to bring out the worst in me for some reason. I assure you I'm the most ordinary creature alive."

He shook his head, but the smile lingered in his curious light eyes. "Then I don't know what you consider ordinary. You rescued a bloody and half-dead stranger from the roadside, saved his life, and now attend to his every need as if it were the most natural thing in the world. And all without self-consciousness or the embarrassment that could so easily make this impossible for both of us. I call that pretty remarkable."

She stopped to consider it, her head to one side in a way she had whenever confronted by a new idea. "Well, I had decided it was you who were responsible for that," she said frankly. "In fact, I had half-dreaded your return to consciousness for just that reason. But it would be pretty ridiculous to be embarrassed by something neither of us can help, don't you think so?"

"Indubitably. But that wouldn't stop most of the Englishwomen of my acquaintance from investing the situation with all the trappings of extreme impropriety."

"Yes, but most Englishwomen can invest a chance meeting in the high street with impropriety," she said with more vehemence than she had intended to reveal.

"Ah, I detect another key to the mystery," he said, teasing her. "You revealed real feeling there."

"Since you are obviously feeling so much stronger," she countered, "I think it's more than time you answered some questions yourself."

She thought his eyes took on a certain wariness, but his smile did not falter. "Ask away, then. My life's an open book."

"I wonder why I doubt that. But your name would do for a start."

He did look startled at that. "Good Lord! I hadn't considered . . . But of course my pockets were completely empty, weren't they? In that case, it was even braver of you to take me in than I'd thought. My name is Rhys Fitzwarren, for what it's worth."

She thought it suited him. "Well, that sounds respectable enough. And what were you doing shot and left for dead on a public road?"

His eyes narrowed, as if for a moment he had forgotten her presence. Then he said lightly, "Ah, there's the mystery. I was held up and robbed in broad daylight and then shot when they were dissatisfied with the pickings. England must have grown a great deal less civilized since last I was here."

"And you are a pronounced prevaricator," she told him. "Don't forget we stripped you, and found the money you had hidden. Why didn't you give it up to save your life? I certainly would have."

"But I didn't know then that they meant to shoot me," he protested plaintively.

She frowned a little at so glib an explanation, but thought better of pushing him any further. "And the foreign climes?" she asked curiously instead.

"Equally unromantic, I fear. I quarreled with my father—one last time—six years ago, and departed in search of adventure."

"And did you find it?"

"Enough. But fair is fair. I've answered your questions. Now it's my turn."

She smiled involuntarily. "At least I hope your questions are more practical than the last time."

"Oh, eminently practical. You now know my name, but all I know is that your given name is Alessia—a provocative-enough fact, I hope you'll agree. And since I am *not* as impudent as your maid seems to think me, I have carefully refrained from addressing you as such, much as I'd like to. What is your surname, and why are you christened with such a deliciously Italian name?"

"You are obviously incorrigible. But my full name is Alessia Fielding, and I have an Italian name for the simple reason that I was born in Italy and my mother was Italian. And you have called me Alessia—or don't you remember?" she teased him.

He groaned. "Obviously in a fever. You can't hold that against me."

"And at least it is more respectable than 'Angel,' which you have also called me," she added severely.

"Yes, but I refuse even to apologize for that. It's obvious you are my guardian angel. You are also trying to change the subject. But I am no longer delirious, nor am I to be fobbed off any longer. You expect me to accept as natural that I find a beautiful, obviously gently-bred girl tending my every need, but I assure you I haven't been out of England *that* long. Even if your father did die six months ago—you see, I remember everything you've told me—there should be cousins and aunts and uncles by the score to keep you from such unconventional situations as this. There is clearly some mystery here, unless . . . Oh, God! What a fool I've been! The one thing I hadn't thought of! You're married, which would explain the lack of chaperone or supervision."

She was amused at his nonsense, but resisted telling him the truth for a moment longer. "No, I'm not married."

"Thank God for that at least!"

"I won't ask you why you thank God so fervently. But though you are the one who should be answering questions, I can see you will get no rest until I tell you. So if you must know, for once I have managed to escape the score of aunts and uncles and cousins. And you can't know how wonderful it feels."

6

He gave a shout of laughter, then swore and clutched his aching side. "Blast these cracked ribs of mine! But I knew you were an unusual girl the moment I set eyes on you. Have you really run away from home?"

She smiled in sympathy at his obvious enjoyment, but said hard-heartedly, "It serves you right for laughing at me. And I should see that you're resting, instead of allowing you to distract me again with your nonsense."

"I seem to have done nothing but sleep lately. And you can't stop there after so provocative a statement."

She sighed, but then settled in a chair by his side and asked curiously, "Would you be shocked if I had?"

"Not in the least. I did, didn't I? Have you?"

"No—though you can't know how often I've longed to in the last six months. But I have taken French leave, for no one knows where I am for the moment."

He was still smiling, but she thought his eyes had grown rather searching. But all he said, and that lightly, was, "Ah, at last we come to the reason for Potton's disapproval of me. And why the last six months? Oh, your father's death, of course," he answered his own question.

She leaned her chin on her hand, another habit of hers when she was thoughtful. "Yes. As for Potton, she does disapprove, but she would never betray me. And although it did start with Papa's death, I now think it had been brewing for a long time before that. But I don't know how I can expect you to understnd. You're a man, and obviously used to doing exactly as you wish, so you can't know just how *desperate* I was feeling."

"I detect a world of resentment in those words! I may be a man, but I hope I'm not so insensitive as not to see it wouldn't be different for a woman," he said sympathetically. "If I had had to be forever surrounded by chaperones and disapproving parents, I think I would have run away myself long before."

"Yes, that's it exactly," she said gratefully. "Only it's ten times worse now, because Papa never bothered with such nonsense. You can't know what it's like to have to account for every minute of my day—especially after being my own mistress for so many years."

"The . . . er . . . aunts and cousins and uncles, I take it?"

"Yes, though luckily I hadn't any aunts and uncles, but only one cousin to annoy me. And Henry has no real power over me, for I have control of my own fortune. But at his insistence I was forced to hire a companion for propriety's sake, to make it possible for me to live on my own in the dower house. And unfortunately she's ten times worse than he is."

"But then, if you managed to convince them to let you live on your own, I congratulate you. That seems sufficiently revolutionary to me."

"Yes, you'd think I'd suggested I should set up my own in the middle of London, or become a hermit in a cottage by the sea! But it had been obvious to me for years that my cousin's wife and I could never live in the same house together. Only

I think now I was never meant to live with *any* other woman."

"You surprise me. I take it the companion did not turn out to be sympathetic?" he asked, grinning.

She sighed. "No. Worse, she's always *there*, chattering about her day and asking me about mine—wanting to make herself useful and instead managing to annoy me a dozen times an hour. But I'm being unfair to Clarissa. She honestly tries to be pleasant and . . . and to enter into my interests. It's not her fault that she's incredibly foolish and talks incessantly of nothing, until I'm ready to scream with vexation."

"My dear child! Say no more. I have met her counterpart all over the world. She cannot endure silence of any form, and so feels it her personal duty to banish any possibility of peace or rational thought in her presence. She prefaces her inanities by a little titter to call attention to herself, and is constantly making apologies for intruding herself upon you. So profound a knowledge of her own folly does not, however, seem to prevent her from ever opening her mouth, as you might think it would. She is also unnaturally inquisitive, and demands to know everything you're doing and thinking, but always with the air of sacrificing herself to your interests. Am I right?"

She laughed despite herself. "Completely. I can laugh at it all now, but I suspect that's only because I've had six weeks away from her company."

"What? She actually let you spend six weeks without her? Hardly wise on her part."

"Yes, but only because my cousin Jane—Henry's wife—needed her more. Yous ee, I haven't told you the worst yet. She spies on me, and reports to Jane, who then reports to Henry, who thinks it his business, as head of the family, to stick his nose into everything I do. I can't direct the gardener to move a bush, or make bramble jelly without one of them offering me advice and direction, usually in direct contravention of what I want to do."

"Yes, it all sounds dreadfully incestuous. But, my sweet idiot, it seems to me there is a simple-enough solution to your problem. In fact you mentioned it yourself."

"I can see it will do me absolutely no good to remind you that such a form of address is extremely improper. And if there's a solution, I'll admit I haven't seen it yet."

"Then you are an idiot. You say, rightly, that you can't live with another woman. Why don't you marry and put an end to Jane's—and Clarissa's—domination over you? I can't believe there aren't a dozen suitors waiting in the wings. In fact I find it hard to believe such a prize wasn't snatched up long ago."

A touch of color ran up her cheeks, but after a moment she said merely, "But then, you are still clearly suffering from fever. And if you mean to imply it is only unmarried females who are at the mercy of others, you are also naive. It seems to me that to marry would merely be exchanging one form of tyranny for another. And I have learned enough of traps in the last six months to be wary of walking blindly into another."

When he laughed out loud again, she looked up, her own eyes alight with amusement. "And that sounded worse than I meant it to. But you seem in some mysterious way to provoke me to say all the things I shouldn't, and have bottled up for so long."

"My child, you're likely to explode one day if you continue to bottle up your emotions, don't you know that? Although if you mean to liken honorable matrimony to slavery, I can see your views would not be popular in polite company."

"Extremely unpopular. And I'm not a child, you know. I was six-and-twenty on my last birthday. You'd think I'd be old enough to run my own life, wouldn't you?"

"Well, even six-and-twenty is not such a great age. And the world seems determined to prevent us from running our own lives. Why do you think I ran away?"

"Is that why? Then I do envy you. And perhaps that's why I'm boring you with all this. You do understand."

"Oh, yes, I understand," he said carelessly. "And you're telling me because it's safe to do so. We're strangers, and this is a moment out of time, not part of either of our lives. It's natural enough."

Her slight frown cleared. "Yes, that's it exactly!"

He was still watching her in an odd way, but he prompted, "But then, you obviously did escape, if only for a while."

"Yes. Luckily an old school friend had just married and moved away, and invited me to visit her. And even more luckily, Jane's two daughters had just come down with the mumps, and so Clarissa was torn between duties. On the one hand, neither approved of my traveling a mere hundred miles on my own, even accompanied by my maid and two grown men to protect me. But neither did she care to leave Jane to cope with the crisis alone."

Then she made a face. "Oh, Lord. You see how old-maidish I've become, when I can be glad two little girls come down with the mumps. And that's my worst fear. Not that I won't learn to put up with Clarissa in time. Of course I will. Nor that I can't ignore Jane's ill will and Henry's condescending kindness. But that I shall grow so . . . so bitter and unhappy I shall end up just like them."

"You are in the mopes," he said teasingly. "But if it's any consolation to you, I find it highly unlikely."

"Thank you, but it's all too likely. Escaping, even for six weeks, has made me see how trapped I have let myself become—and how much it has affected my temper. Sometimes it is all I can do to be polite to poor Clarissa—and if I've made her seem an ogre, I've done her less than justice. She means well. She just—"

"Never mind!" he interrupted in amusement. "Those three words could be used to sum up most of the bunglers and fools who make our lives miserable. *They mean well.* That doesn't excuse them for being insensitive and boring and all-round nuisances."

"No. Perhaps not. But driving home, I was almost desperate. I know now that I should get completely away, but I don't know how I can. Now that I'm settled into the dower house, it would look as if Henry and Jane had driven me away. I don't think I'd let even that stop me if I knew where to go, but I don't. Unfortunately, much as I might like to, I can't run off to the Continent to enjoy adventures as you did. Or at least, not the kind of adventures I have in mind," she added dryly.

He grinned at her. "You're right, I fear. But what sort of adventures do you have in mind?"

"I don't know, which makes it even more absurd. No doubt very mild ones, to your way of thinking. To travel on my own, without all the constraints of a suitable chaperone and grooms and maids and footmen, all watching out after me as if I were some delicate hothouse flower. To be spontaneous for once in my life, without considering other people's demands and meekly bowing down to them. To do what I want, not what other people expect me to do." She looked up self-consciously, torn between embarrassment and laughter. "I told you it would sound a pitiful-enough list."

"On the contrary. Those are the most important things of all. And you were clearly due for a rebellion. I only wish I could offer you a better one than this."

"Yes, but you can have no conception of how much I've enjoyed even this last week, which shows you just how desperate I'd become. I've been free, you see. No one knows where I am, and I can do exactly as I like."

"My poor Angel! I don't think much of the freedom to sit up all night nursing a perfect stranger who was fool enough to allow himself to be left for dead in the snow," he said ruefully.

"Yes, even that. It's made me see . . . Oh, I don't know what. I am brave enough now, but I fear when it comes to the point, I shall meekly give in again. I never used to think I was such an abysmal coward, but then, I doubt one does of oneself."

"My sweet, anyone can be brave in battle. It's only when faced with the emotional blackmail and threat of social disapproval that others use to keep us in line that most of us fall short."

"Is it?" she asked wonderingly. "Perhaps you're right. But I was thinking about all this when we found you. In fact, I'd just been fervently wishing that *something* would happen to keep me from having to go home again. And then there you were."

He grinned lazily across at her. "Almost like the answer to a prayer. In that case I'm glad I was able to be of some service—however passive."

She looked up quickly, her face alight with sudden warm laughter. "Yes, I hoped you would be.

I'm not saying you had yourself shot and left for dead just to oblige me, but I'm grateful to you anyway."

"Yes, and this is all very well, but what have you told the estimable Henry and Jane about your absence? If they were ever to guess the real reason, you'd be in far worse trouble, I fear."

"Well, I may admittedly be new at this kind of subterfuge, but I'm not in the least stupid. In fact, you may not know it, but I am that most deplorable of all feminine creatures, a bluestocking, so be warned. My father was the noted Sir William Fielding, the authority on Dante," she told him in amusement. "I merely sent a message that my friend had at the last minute asked me to accompany her on a trip she was planning. And before you can point out the obvious flaw in that plan, I should tell you that Theresa really was leaving on a trip to visit her mother-in-law, so she won't be home to receive any urgent messages from my cousin or his wife."

"Ah, I congratulate you. Masterly planning. So, having freed yourself—however briefly—of all chaperones and disapproving relations, what do you intend to do with your freedom? I must confess that staying in an inferior inn, sleeping days, and tending an annoying invalid hardly seem like a holiday to me."

"Yes, but you can't know how boring my days are usually," she countered. "And I don't suppose I intend to do anything. I . . . well, I was confronted with a mortally ill man whom no one else wanted to take responsibility for. And since I had just been wishing for an adventure, it seemed ungrateful for me to turn you over to someone else and weakly trot home again. Potton disapproves, but she won't betray me, and James and Horsham—the coachmen—have known me all my life. So you see, I'm not taking much of a risk."

"On the contrary. You are taking an enormous risk," he said, only half-teasingly. "Or haven't you discovered that yet?"

When she looked puzzled, he added mockingly, "Freedom is amazingly seductive, I fear. I should know. You may discover that by taking this seemingly tiny step you're tempting more fates than you know."

Her brow cleared. "I only wish I might find it so. I fear far more than I shall meekly go back, when the time comes, and accept my fate. I warned you that for all my complaints, I have discovered I am a shocking coward."

He made no comment, but regarded her oddly for several long moments. Then he smiled and said lightly, "Then I clearly shall have to see what I can do about that, won't I? It's the least I can do to repay you for saving my life."

7

After Alessia's confession, the patient seemed to improve with dramatic rapidity. The next day he insisted upon dispensing with the round-the-clock attendance, and further irritated Potton by having himself shaved.

He was still obviously weak, but by the tenth day he was on his feet and demanding to be entertained.

He complained of the tight band binding his ribs, but had consented to a light sling for his arm. After that it was impossible to keep him quiet. He roamed the inn, was prevented only by the continuance of bad weather from venturing outdoors, and generally refused to be treated anymore as an invalid.

Once Alessia complained, as she was rebinding his ribs for him. "You could be more grateful, you know. If you insist upon recovering so quickly, I shall have no excuse but to return home again."

His quick, infectious grin showed. "Then I shall take to my bed again without delay. But you know, having gained your freedom, you have no need to abandon it so quickly. You may as well be hanged for a sheep as a lamb."

She sighed and finished her tasks. "There. Don't wriggle so or you'll make it come loose again. You're as bad as a little boy. Yes, but it must end soon, you know. Once you are well again, my conscience will have no other excuse to put off the inevitable."

He was shrugging into his shirt again, but he eyed

her quickly. "Have you enjoyed these past few days, Angel?"

"You don't know how much," she said truthfully. In truth she was sometimes amazed at how comfortable she felt in his company. For all the embarrassment either of them seemed to feel in their enforced intimacy, they might have been friends since childhood, or even brother and sister.

Sometimes, in her bedchamber at night, Alessia pondered on exactly why that should be so, but could never quite put her finger on the answer. Rhys was an amusing companion of course; seldom serious and treating her in many ways like the brother she'd never had. He allowed her to dress his wound, complained bitterly if she pulled it too tight or stuck a pin into his tender flesh, teased her, and disobeyed her severe orders not to overdo.

He also called her Angel and flattered her outrageously, but never once had he betrayed any awareness of the fact that they were a man and a woman thrust together in a most unconventional intimacy. She might indeed have been his younger sister.

The fact piqued her sometimes, but she knew that if he had ever once stepped over that line she would have had to leave immediately.

And she was strangely loath to end this unexpected idyll.

She discovered he was still watching her, but he said merely, "I always said you were woefully easy to please."

"Perhaps. But you see, I don't think I ever had a real friend before."

He looked briefly startled at than, then oddly rueful for some reason. "What, none?"

She put her head to one side as she always did

when serious. "Oh, schoolgirl acquaintances, of course. Local friends one meets and likes in a vague sort of way. But at the risk of making you even vainer than you already are, never one who made me laugh as you do, and wasn't shocked by anything I might say or do. Perhaps if I'd had a brother or sister—or a cousin I was close to—it might have been different."

He had turned to stare out the window at the dismal prospect of freezing rain. "Perhaps. I had a cousin once who was a good friend. But I know what you mean. Good friends are rare enough."

"What happened to him? Your cousin, I mean?"

He did turn at that, looking rakish with his arm in a sling and his shirt left unbuttoned across his chest. Alessia knew that Henry would be shocked to see them together like that. "He was a far more dutiful son than I was. I haven't heard much of him since I left six years ago."

"He must be married and with a family by now."

He looked startled at her remark. "Good God! I must confess I hadn't thought of that!"

"Careful. You're unwittingly betraying your attitude toward matrimony. Would that be so awful?"

"For him, no. In fact I think it would suit him very well."

She laughed then. "But for you it would be disastrous. You needn't say it."

He had the slow grin in his eyes that she so much appreciated. "Oh, not disastrous. Let's just say I haven't given it much thought."

"Do you never intend to marry, then?" she asked curiously. She knew she should roll up her bandages and withdraw, but she had grown into the custom of treating his room very much as her own.

"Never is a very long time. And for one who just a few days ago was likening matrimony to slavery, you've little room to talk."

"But then, I'm convinced marriage is a very different proposition for me. You, after all, don't endow your wife with all your worldly goods and promise to obey until death do you part."

"Come now. I've seen far too many husbands tied meekly to their wives' apron strings to believe that."

She sighed, choosing to treat their nonsense seriously. "Yes, but it seems to me that's very little better. A partnership, in which both appreciated and respected each other, would be different, but how rare that seems to be."

"Did your parents have such a partnership?"

She looked up quickly, then shrugged. "I don't know. My mother died before I was old enough to really remember her. I'm told I have her looks and something of her temperament, but I can't really judge. I've never even seen a portrait of her."

"Do you remember Italy at all?"

"Oh, yes! At least, I think I do, though sometimes I wonder if I'm not just imagining it. I remember the sun always shining, and oranges growing in the garden, warm and juicy. And I have never liked the cold—which must be from my Italian roots. But very little more, I'm afraid."

He smiled. "Little enough of half your heritage. How did your father come to marry an Italian woman?"

Again she looked up, but saw nothing but lazy interest in his face. "He was a scholar of some repute, as I told you. He devoted his life to translating Dante into English, so I daresay it was natural for him to travel to Italy. They met and married, and so he stayed, at least until she died. Then I think he could never bear to go back, though

I've often wondered how he could leave it all behind to return to cold, wet England."

"Ah, spoken like a true Italian!" he teased her. "But you're right. Italy's an enchanting place. The sea is warm and the sky always blue, and the people warm and passionate. They never speak rationally when shouting would serve them better, and spend their days either making love or fighting. They find the English a dour, cold lot, I'm afraid."

"Yes, yes!" she said eagerly. "I remember the noise; and the easy affection of my nurse and all her many relatives. We must have gone to visit them once, in the country, for I remember everyone grabbing me up and hugging and kissing me. I can't imagine such a thing happening in England."

"No. We're far too cold-blooded for that."

"Yes. How I'd like to go back someday. But I might as well aim for the moon. But what of your mother?" she asked curiously. "Was she still alive when you left?"

She had asked him very little about his past, and he had volunteered little more. He had once or twice described some of his travels, and she had found herself enchanted, and envied his freedom with all her heart. But he seldom spoke of his life before he'd left England six years ago.

He shrugged now. "No, like yours, she died when I was scarcely old enough to remember her. But at least my father was by no means cold-blooded. We quarreled on any and all occasions, I'm afraid."

Then he grinned at her. "But enough of this gloomy talk! You owe me a scandalous amount at whist, and are obviously trying to distract me from our daily game."

"Scandalous is right," she grumbled as she obediently rose to fetch the cards. "No one should win as consistently as you do."

He felt instinctively for the ring, now safely on a chain around his neck again. "I told you I've always been phenomenally lucky. Let's see if your luck has changed for once."

She suspected he let her win, and bitterly accused him of the fact. He laughed and denied it, and in the end she retired to bed very much on her dignity.

But it was not to sleep. She lay there oddly contented, thinking that she had told him the simple truth earlier. She had discovered she had little experience of the free-and-easy companionship they now enjoyed. Her father had been a serious man, more interested in pursuing an elusive Italian translation than sharing jests with his only daughter. She had helped him with his work, and come to enjoy it for her own sake as well as his; but she supposed now she had led a strange, isolated childhood.

It was not that her father had forbidden her to make friendships or do whatever she pleased. But since he himself needed no one, he had taken it for granted that she would be the same, and somehow she had followed his unconscious lead.

Her experience of living with Clarissa had only reinforced that notion, for within herself she had secretly feared there must be something wrong with her. It seemed she was so used to her own company, and the companionable silences she and her father enjoyed, that she was unfit for living with anyone else. It had even affected her attitude toward matrimony; for if at the end of six months she was ready to murder Clarissa, whom she could escape if she chose, and even dismiss if necessary, how much worse would it be to try living with a husband?

But Rhys had inadvertently showed her her

mistake. In almost a fortnight of living in the closest intimacy with him, she had given no single thought to her own need for privacy. She woke eagerly every morning and went to sleep at night pleasurably tired, content to know that her amusing friend would be there waiting for her. It was no wonder she shied from looking beyond the moment, and why she dreaded his full recovery.

Unfortunately the idyll was to end even sooner than she feared, for when she went downstairs the next morning, in search of the fat landlord, Ditchling, it was to find a stranger in the taproom. Usually at that early hour she could rely on finding the landlord setting things to rights after the previous night's custom. Ditchling had, by and large, proved a tolerant if overworked landlord, and had given the entire use of his house over to her without a murmur.

But this time he was nowhere in sight, and a solitary customer stood at the bar, still heavily cloaked against the cold.

He looked around as she came in, and she was annoyed at her carelessness. She was close enough to her home to fear meeting someone who knew her, and usually took good care to stay out of sight of any inquisitive strangers.

But it was too late to draw back, and so she came on into the room, saying pleasantly, "I was looking for the landlord. Have you seen him?"

There was something about the newcomer's looks she didn't like, but he raised his hat politely enough. "I was just wondering the same," he said, his voice thick with a cold. "But happen you can help me instead."

A quarter of an hour later Alessia quickly entered

Rhys' bedchamber and shut the door behind her, her face unnaturally pale and her hands far from steady.

He had been engaged in a game of one-handed whist, but looked around as she came in and gave her the smile that never failed to make her pulse stir. "Ah, there you are! I was afraid you were really offended and meant to leave me to my own devices today."

Then he took in her agitated manner and his face altered immediately. "Angel! What is it? You *aren't* still angry with me, are you?"

"No, no, of course not! I . . ." She drew a shaky breath, wanting suddenly to put off the moment. But it was far too late for that. "There's a man downstairs looking for you," she blurted.

He stiffened, but his expression did not alter. "For me? I doubt it. Few people know I'm back in England."

"Oh, don't bother to keep up the polite excuses!" she cried agitatedly. "It seems he's discovered you're not dead after all. And I very much fear he means to correct that oversight!"

8

For a moment Rhys stood regarding her steadily, his expression giving nothing away. Then he shrugged and asked quietly, "How long have you suspected?"

"Almost from the beginning. You cried out once or twice in your delirium. And common highwaymen don't usually rob their victims and then shoot them and leave them for dead, at least not in England."

"What did I say?" he asked, a touch of grimness creeping into his tone.

"Nothing much that I could understand. You seemed relieved that they hadn't found your talisman, is all. Is that what they were looking for?"

His hand automatically went to his chest to finger the gold ring there, and then he grimaced. "It would seem so. But what of the man downstairs?"

"I think I managed to convince him for the moment. I told him my maid had been taken ill, and I had been here almost a fortnight and had certainly heard nothing of any wounded man. It was only fortunate I went down this morning in search of Ditchling and he was out of the room at the time. But I'm afraid we can't rely on someone else not talking and something must have drawn him here. And they obviously know now that you're not dead."

He grinned crookedly. "Yes, I thought it was careless of them not to make sure they'd finished me off. And it seems I am now doubly in your debt, Angel."

She brushed that aside. "Don't be ridiculous. Only, while I don't like to appear vulgarly inquisitive, I confess I would like to know why someone is trying so hard to do away with you."

"Unfortunately, the honest truth is that I just don't know," he admitted ruefully. "I had almost managed to convince myself that it was a case of mistaken identity after all."

She stared at him, feeling her sense of unreality growing. "Someone shot you and left you for dead, and has now returned to try to finish his handiwork, and you . . . don't . . . know . . . *why*?"

"Absurd, isn't it? What did the man downstairs look like, by the way?"

"Dark. Not tall, but powerfully built. He made my blood run cold, as a matter of fact," she answered, shivering a little even now. "He also had a bad cold."

"Yes, that sounds like one of them."

"Are you telling me you'd never seen either of them before?"

"Never."

"And you've absolutely no idea why they might want to kill you?"

He grinned at her. "Believe me, I had ample time as I lay out in the snow to think about it. I suppose there's always the chance, as you so indelicately once hinted to me, that it was a father or husband with an exceedingly long memory. But somehow I don't think so. For one thing, I returned to the country only two days before I was attacked, and only one or two people knew I was back. And for another, I can't think of any likely candidate in my admittedly far-from-blameless past. I can't even think of anyone—outside of my father—who had any kind of a grudge against me, or whom I've wronged, no matter how inadvertently."

Her brow cleared slightly. "Then it could be a mistake! They've obviously mistaken you for someone else."

"Unfortunately they don't seem willing to wait while I straighten out the mix-up."

"But this is incredible. It's like something out of a novel."

"I agree. And a poor one at that. Unfortunately, several things they said as I lay in the snow and they obviously thought me beyond taking anything in led me to believe they were indeed looking for me—or someone enough like me to be my double. They had had a description of me from the inn I'd stayed at the night before, you see. They also spent considerable time searching my baggage for something."

"Your ring!" she whispered in a scared voice.

"It would seem so. It's known I never go anywhere without it. Luckily I had put it away on a chain for safekeeping on the road. I have grown used to being safe rather than sorry where it is concerned. I fear I'm ridiculously superstitious about it."

Then he grimaced. "Although it may have betrayed me this time. I can't think those two were thorough enough on their own to come back and make sure I was dead. Whoever hired them must have refused to take their word for my death until they had produced the proof he wanted."

She shuddered. "But you must have some idea who could want you dead so badly."

"You'd think so, wouldn't you?" he answered cheerfully. "But I keep telling you, only one or two persons even knew I was back in England. And I can't quite see old Kettlewell hiring an assassin to waylay me. He has never approved of me, admittedly, but apart from every other consideration, he has absolutely no motive for getting rid of me."

"But someone must have," she insisted.

"Yes, that's the absurd part. But then, everything has seemed odd since I've been back," he admitted more slowly. "I came, as I told you, because I'd belatedly gotten word of my father's death. It took three months for the letter to reach me, and another six weeks before I could get back. I was . . . er . . . in a rather inacessible place at the time. I came out of a sense of duty, admittedly not wanting the inheritance I expected to find. But I was still startled when Kettlewell informed me that my father had rewritten his will in the last six months and disinherited me completely."

"But if you had quarreled so bitterly . . . ?"

"We had quarreled, yes, but I think I told you we frequently fought about anything and everything. My father was a stiff-necked old devil with outmoded notions of conduct and duty, and I'll admit I was enough to try anyone's patience. I refused to give in to the life he had planned for me, and he in turn threatened regularly to cut me off with a shilling. But I must admit I never really expected him to do it."

Then he shrugged. "But then, the one thing we consistently quarreled about was his obsession about Crickfield—my less-than-ancestral home. I never had any desire to be saddled with so great a monstrosity and all his antiquated notions of *droit de seigneur* and *noblesse oblige*, and he knew it."

His eyes seemed to be seeing things she couldn't, and he continued, almost to himself. "Nor did his anger generally last long, to do him credit. We had had a dozen more serious quarrels before I finally walked out, all of which blew over. And it had blown over! We by no means carried on a regular correspondence—I was usually too inaccessible for that. But I heard from him only a few months before he made his new will, and his letter was perfectly civil. He still damned my eyes for having run out on my responsibilities, and threw my cousin Owen's virtues up to me. But he was obviously reconciled to my absence."

"Could he have finally realized you didn't want the inheritance, then?"

"Obviously so, though that was the last thing I would have said he'd allow to weigh with him. I told you he had exceedingly outmoded ideas about family honor and property being handed on from father to son. Like you, I'm not inexperienced when it comes to suffering from the demands of primogeniture."

"Whom did he leave the property to, if not you?" she asked curiously.

"My Uncle Walter—and ultimately my virtuous cousin Owen." Then he grinned. "And before you begin imagining anything sinister in that, I should correct what is undoubtedly an exaggerated view of my so-called 'inheritance.' It consists of one estate that hasn't paid its way for years, and is a drain rather than an asset, and a houseful of uncomfortable and outmoded furnishings. Only my father would have fought so long to keep it intact."

"Yes, but you haven't been back in six years. I suppose it could have increased in value."

"I only wish it might have—for my uncle's sake. But Kettlewell would have been bound to have told me. There seems to be no doubt that the will is genuine, so they could hardly fear my trying to overset it. Kettlewell seemed to be surprised I'd bothered to return at all. Evidently he wrote a second letter after the first, that never reached me, informing me of the terms of the will. And if you are picturing him in the role of a conspirator, you obviously haven't seen him. He's eighty, slightly deaf, and still treats me as if I were in shortcoats."

She managed to smile, though it didn't quite reach her eyes. "Nevertheless the fact remains that someone tried to have you murdered—not once, but twice. Could . . . could the ring itself be the reason? Perhaps it's worth far more than you know."

"Only in sentimental value. It belonged to my maternal grandfather. He was always superstitious about it, and immediately after he left it to me, I was saved from breaking my neck over a rasper only by the sheerest fluke. Since then I've never cared to be without it. But it's no more than fifty years old, and doesn't even have a valuable stone. It can't be that."

"It couldn't . . . have a secret compartment or some kind of code engraved on it that would mean something to someone else, but nothing to you?" she suggested, feeling foolish even as she did so.

"I doubt it, but I'll admit I hadn't thought of that. Anything's worth trying, I suppose."

He obligingly produced his ring and removed it from the chain, then handed it to her, himself hampered by his sling.

She took it eagerly, but at the end of fifteen minutes of poking and prying at it was forced to concede unwilling defeat. "It seems to be a ring, no more and no less. Could there be anything in the crest? A sort of secret code to buried treasure or the like?"

She could tell he was finding the whole extremely entertaining, but he shrugged at that. "The coat of arms is from my mother's family, and seems perfectly normal. But I suppose it could be a key of some kind."

"There could be a fortune in gold hidden in a

secret compartment behind a painted version of the family coat of arms, for instance," she offered, getting into the spirit of the thing. "Or—"

"Buried in the center of a maze laid out in the exact same pattern! Unfortunately, so far as I know, no such maze exists, and my maternal relations are numerous. I can't help thinking that even if such a treasure did exist, they would know far more about it than I would."

Alessia turned the ring over one last time, then handed it back in frustration. "Yes, and if the ring is indeed an exact duplicate of the family crest, they would hardly need it."

He hesitated, then slipped the ring on his finger. "There is that as well. In fact I can't help thinking that if I were indeed the intended victim, its value lay in the fact it was known I would never willingly stir without it. But there I stick. I can't imagine that I'm important enough to anyone to warrant an attempt to remove me."

She looked up, then quickly back down again. He caught it, and said in amusement, "Go on! If you've any more suggestions, I'd be glad to hear them."

Still she hesitated. "But I've no wish to offend you, so perhaps I should say no more."

He grinned. "Good God, don't let that stop you. I haven't any sensibilities for you to offend."

She wondered. The solution seemed fairly obvious to her, and yet he hadn't reached it, which told its own tale. "Yes, but I've no idea how fond you may be of your relatives—your paternal ones, that is."

He looked genuinely surprised. "Of my uncle, not at all. Of my cousin Owen, I used to be fond of him, but that was many years ago. The rest I seldom saw even as a child, and cared even less about."

"Then I can't help thinking that there must be

something in the inheritance you dismiss so lightly that makes someone willing to . . . kill to get it."

He burst out laughing. "I only wish it were! Believe me, that was my first thought, too. But I find it impossible to believe."

"Why?" she demanded bluntly. "Because you know your relatives are incapable of such an act, or you find it hard to believe an estate you once held in contempt could have increased in value?"

"You certainly don't pull your punches, do you? Both, I suppose. Or perhaps neither. My uncle and I were never close, so I've no idea what he's capable of. I've never particularly liked him, but that doesn't make him a murderer. As for the estate, all the land that might have made it at least self-supporting was sold off when I was a boy. There's nothing left but a moldering pile that should be torn down and left as a monument to undeserved family pride. Even if my uncle were capable of murder, it wouldn't be for that pile of worthless bricks and mortar, believe me."

He sounded convinced. "Then . . . something within the house," she suggested, clutching at straws.

"What, more hidden treasure?" He grinned appreciatively at the thought. "I'm willing enough to consign my uncle to the role of nephew-murderer for the sake of argument, but surely if that were so, he had only to remove the treasure, not murder me. He has, after all, had a number of months in which to do so."

"But perhaps he hasn't found it yet! And the talisman ring is somehow a clue."

He burst out laughing at that. "Which will be revealed only when the light of the new moon shines on it in the proper month. But if my father is supposed to have hidden the treasure, which he would have had to do, for he bought the house when

I was a child, I fear I have even more objections. He scrabbled for money all his life to feed his obsession about Crickfield. He would hardly have left that unspent."

"Well, then, something else in the house—something that not even he knew he possessed. An unknown masterpiece, or a document signed by William the Conqueror; or . . . or a rare set of books. You probably don't realize how valuable books can be, and, more important, neither would your father unless he were a scholar. But somehow your uncle found out, and bided his time until your father died."

"The same objection holds, I'm afraid," he said regretfully, "Why didn't he merely remove the books or sell the painting before I arrived? Come to that, if my father didn't know what he had, my uncle might have safely removed it years ago. No, I must confess I'm growing enamored of the idea of my uncle as chief villain in the piece. It's so incongruous, I can't resist. But I can see no reason for him to try to murder me. I can hardly be a threat to him."

"I have an answer for that. He might fear you would recognize the painting—or whatever—once it had been sold."

"But the fact still remains that it all belongs to him now. He can sell whatever he likes."

"Not if he feared you would try to overset the will," she produced triumphantly.

"I'm sorry. But you are being rather absurd, you know, my sweet idiot. And it's particularly unkind in you to make me laugh so much in my delicate condition."

"But then I didn't find the ball we dug out of your side as amusing as you obviously do," she pointed out.

"Ouch! Very well, I concede the point. And I'll

admit it does rather rankle, for I'm as attached to my skin as the next fellow."

It was obvious he was not taking it nearly as seriously as she was. She said after a moment, in a voice she did her best to keep steady, "At least you do realize that we . . . shall have to leave here now?"

He regarded her sympathetically. "Yes, and for that I'm genuinely sorry. It seems your stolen holiday is at an end. I only hope you found it worthwhile."

She doubted he would ever know just how much these last stolen weeks had meant to her, and no doubt it was better that way. "Yes, it is more than time I went home again," she said quietly. "You were right. Freedom is oddly seductive. But what do you intend to do?"

"I don't know. Go on to Crickfield, I guess, and see if my uncle is surprised to have me turn up."

"And if he is the one plotting against you, give him the leisure to choose the time and place to finish you off?" she asked bitterly.

He frowned a little. "Good Lord, you are taking it seriously, aren't you, Angel? I assure you I'm remarkably difficult to kill."

"What you are is remarkably obtuse!" Renewed fear made her voice unnaturally sharp. "It is amusing to joke about, but I'm not in the habit of finding bodies under the wheels of my carriage. Nor, having nursed you back to health, do I care to see my handiwork go to waste."

He still looked amused, but remained silent. After a moment she added in a voice that brooked no argument, "But I'll tell you exactly what you are going to do. Horsham, my cousin's coachman, has an extra room in his cottage. You're going to go there, at least until you are strong enough to take care of yourself."

9

Still Rhys said nothing. Then at last he said wryly, "And thus speaks the consumate coward. But I've involved you too much already."

"But I *am* involved. At any rate, however much you try to hide the fact, I am perfectly aware you are not as strong as you pretend. Your ribs still pain you, and you can scarcely lift your right arm at all. What match would you be in your present shape against hired assassins?"

He grimaced, for it was too near the truth for comfort. He was still damnably weak, and he did not tell her how many nights he still spent awake, trying to find a position that allowed him some slight ease.

On the other hand, despite their earlier nonsense, he still could not believe in any of the theories they had produced to date. He had no enemies, and nothing for anyone to gain by murdering him. The whole thing was some absurd mix-up.

As if sensing that he was weakening, she said quickly, "And if you fear that they will be able to trace you through me, I should perhaps tell you that I took the precaution of not using my own name here. It is a little too close to my home for comfort, and so I have carefully used the name of Miss Smith throughout."

He couldn't help it. He burst out laughing. "A wise precaution! But I still should refuse to involve you any further. Have you thought of what you're going to tell Clarissa and Cousin Jane if I come back with you? If you're not careful, all your subterfuge will have been for naught."

"I shan't have to tell them anything," she said sunnily. "Horsham is devoted to me and will do whatever I ask him, and his wife is a kindly creature. They live far enough from the main house for your presence to go unnoticed, and if it is, you can pass yourself off as Horsham's nephew, come to pay him a visit."

"Does Horsham have a nephew?" he inquired in amusement.

"I've no idea. But you can say you've been in the army . . . er . . . batman to an officer, to explain your speech and naffy ways. It won't be for very long at any rate, so you should be able to keep up the masquerade until you've fully recovered."

"Well, I've no objection to passing myself off as Horsham's nephew—even a military one!" he said, grinning. "But I'm afraid that even to do that, I shall have to augment my wardrobe slightly. The bulk of my trunks are still in London, and I lost everything else. I can send for my trunks, of course, but I can hardly go on relying on the goodwill of Mrs. Horsham—however kindly a creature—to wash out my one shirt every night. And I feel sure even . . . er . . . batman would make a better appearance than I do at the moment."

"Horsham will take you into the village to buy new clothes. As for your trunks, I can't help but think it might be best to leave them where they are. If anyone really is determined to find you, he might easily be keeping an eye on them. And if you are worried about being in my debt, I should perhaps tell you that the boot is very much on the other foot," she added frankly. "I long since exhausted what money I had with me, and have been shamelessly dipping into that we found on you. In fact, since under the circumstances I think we should not wait to send for Horsham, but hire a coach locally instead, you will be called upon to pay the posting charges, for my pockets are completely to let. I am dependent upon you to rescue me."

He eyed her appreciatively. "You know you are welcome to whatever I have, so stop trying to change the subject. And *if* I agree to come, it will be on the clear understanding that at the first hint of danger, I leave—fully recovered or no. Is that understood?"

"Perfectly. But I also intend to inform the landlord that we will be taking you only as far as Cheltenham, where you mean to take the stage to London. If our suspicious visitor returns, he will have no choice but to follow. And searching for you in London should keep him busy for some little time, I should think."

He was once more amused, but had to admit that by the end of the relatively brief journey to her home he was longing only to lie down and sleep for a week. His ribs had sustained no good from the endless jolting of the badly sprung carriage, and he could only hold himself stiffly, trying to hide the discomfort he felt.

Alessia regarded this silent suffering with a growing frown between her straight brows, and once said unhappily, "I'm sorry. I should have sent for Horsham after all. This is intolerable!"

He waved that aside, but thankful as he was for the end of the torture, it was all he could do to unbend himself and climb down from the carriage with a modicum of dignity at the journey's end.

Alessia refused his help to descend and went immediately inside to speak with her faithful coachman, the frown still lingering. While Rhys waited, held stiffly erect only with a supreme effort of will, and annoyed with himself for his weakness, he caught the maid Potton's eye on him.

He looked away, at the moment unable to confront the disapproval he read there.

Alessia returned almost immediately, a surprised and even more disapproving Horsham at her back. Rhys recognized the protective instincts of her henchman, and could only applaud them. But at the moment he was simply too spent to worry about anything but getting himself to bed.

He insisted this time on helping Alessia back into the hired coach, and retained her hand once he did so. "It seems wholly inadequate to try to express my thanks, for you know I am eternally in your debt, Angel."

She smiled and tried to defuse the situation. "Nonsense. Anyone would have done as I did."

His own mouth twisted faintly. "I doubt it. But then, you are lamentably backward at recognizing your own virtues. I am only sorry your brief taste of freedom had to come to such an abrupt end."

"It doesn't matter," she said quickly. "It had to end sometime. I have always known that."

"Yes, I suppose so. We must all come down to earth again sometime." He hesitated, then abruptly raised her gloved hand and pressed his lips to the delicate inside of her wrist where the glove left it bare. It was the only such intimate gesture he had ever permitted himself.

"Don't let Clarissa and Cousin Jane get to you too badly, Angel," he said lightly, and let her go.

But as he watched the carriage out of sight, he wondered ruefully if even that slight break in his determination not to take advantage of the absurd situation they found themselves in hadn't been too dangerous.

* * *

After Rhys's impulsive gesture, it was scarcely surprising that Alessia didn't even notice the homecoming she had once so dreaded.

Clarissa, a thin, colorless little woman, almost fell on her neck with cries of joy, and made it plain that she had not spent an easy night since Horsham had delivered that *very* odd note from dearest Alessia.

Alessia discovered she had even less patience than usual for her, for she wanted to be alone with her thoughts. "What on earth was odd about it?" she demanded. "I told you that Theresa was feeling ill and at the last moment begged me to make the journey with her, and I saw no reason to refuse."

Clarissa rushed to appease her. "Oh, no, dearest, of course not. Though if she was feeling all that ill, it seems rather odd that she chose to make the journey anyway. Not that I mean to criticize her, of course. Only, when one is in such a delicate situation, you know, it does seem as if she should take no risks with her health."

"She is increasing, not dying of consumption," retorted Alessia. "I take it Sophie and Amily are fully recovered?"

Clarissa seized gratefully on that topic. "Oh, *yes*, poor things. I'm sure I've never seen anyone suffer so. Often the tears would quite spring to my own eyes, but of course it would never do to let them think I was upset. They were quite frightened enough on their own, and kept crying quite *touchingly* for their mother."

"No, Jane would be of little use in a sickroom," returned Alessia sardonically.

"But of course, she is so *busy*, with all her new duties, though it quite *tortured* her to see her babies so ill. She paid me the compliment of saying she didn't know what she would have done without me."

"No doubt. It is indeed convenient to have someone else perform all one's more onerous tasks."

But sarcasm was always wasted on Clarissa. Alessia had never decided whether she really did not detect a less palatable meaning to some of Alessia's barbs, or merely chose not to. Now she said only, "Oh, yes! So comforting to know that one is useful. Though I have regretted a dozen times a day the necessity that made me abandon you at such a time. I hope you know that I am *quite* aware where my first responsibility lies. Indeed, dearest Lady Fielding flatters me by saying loyalty is my most notable quality. And I do hope she's right, for I have certainly always held it to be a particularly *admirable* quality, haven't you? And now, dearest, I fear I must scold you just a little! You can't know how worried dear Lady Fielding and Sir Henry were to learn you meant to stay away longer than you had planned."

Alessia had to make herself take hold of her temper. "Lady Fielding and Sir Henry also know they have not the least control over what I may choose to do. And since I have existed for some twenty-six years without their assistance, I feel sure I can continue to do so."

"Oh, yes, my dear, but your father was alive then, of course. I mean, little though we may like to acknowledge it, women *are* the weaker sex. No one knows better than I, I assure you, nor sympathizes more with you, for I know it must sometimes feel *odd* to find yourself supplanted and made to feel a guest in your own house. But both Sir Henry and Lady Fielding are extremely fond of you, you know, and indeed would be very hurt if they thought you were not happy here any longer."

As always after spending five minutes in Clarissa's company, Alessia felt the usual annoyed impatience creeping over her. Clarissa clearly meant well, but she had a positive evil genius for touching on wounds too deep to be discussed, and blundering in foolishly where a person with more tact would have known to stay away.

But it did no good to remember the days spent with a far more congenial companion, full of contented silences and shared laughter. So she soon pleaded tiredness as an excuse to escape Clarissa's eager questions, and retired to her bedchamber.

Her respite was unfortunately brief. Jane, with the two girls and Henry in tow, wasted very little time in calling, as she said, to welcome Alessia back; but in reality to cross-examine her about her sudden change in plans.

She was a gaunt, plain woman of little charm and even less tact. She was practical and full of good advice—which she was overfond of dispensing in a voice that ignored any possible objections—and prided herself on her plain speaking. She ruled her meek husband with a rod of iron, spoke dotingly of her two equally plain daughters while spending as little time as possible in their company, and still found time to have her nose in all the affairs of the district.

She greeted Alessia effusively, then questioned her minutely on her visit, on her friend's house, and on her husband's fortune and background. Finding nothing much to complain of there, she at last conceded grudgingly, "Well, she sounds a most obliging girl. Though, mind, I do think it was thoughtless of her to invite you to visit so soon after your poor papa's death."

"But that is precisely the reason she chose to invite me. She thought I could do with a change, and she was right."

Jane's mouth tightened in disapproval, and she

looked her husband's cousin over more carefully, noticing for the first time the subtle change in her. She had never cared for Alessia—outlandish name! She flatly refused to give it credence by using it, and always addressed her as Alice—and was extremely jealous of her beauty and popularity in the neighborhood. It annoyed her that Alessia, half Italian and thus highly suspect in her estimation, as well as being dark as a Gypsy with that strange, almost exotic look of hers, should find such ready acceptance in the neighborhood, while she, far better bred and connected, still was made to feel an outsider.

But it occured to her now that her cousin-in-law was looking particularly blooming, for some reason. Jane's eyes narrowed and she remarked with raised brows, "But I must admit the journey does seem to have agreed with you. Who would have thought a mere visit to an old school friend could have worked such wonders in so short a time."

Alessia merely smiled, but Clarissa put in foolishly, "Oh, yes! I noticed it myself. Of course, dear Alessia is always beautiful, but she looks . . . I don't know! Different somehow. Almost glowing."

Jane glanced at Alessia sharply again, her suspicions growing, but in front of her husband merely contented herself with remarking dryly, "Indeed yes. I am glad the trip was so successful. Which reminds me. That wretched Horsham has invited a nephew of his to stay with him. He very properly came to apprise Henry of the fact, but it seems he might have asked his permission *before* rather than after the fact. He claims the nephew just turned up unexpectedly, and has been out of the country for some years. Batman to an officer, I understand. I really had no idea Horsham aspired to such heights."

10

Alessia had started, but she made herself ask calmly, "Do you have any reson to doubt Horsham?" She poured Henry out another cup of tea, pleased to note her hand was perfectly steady.

"Oh, he was straightforward enough about it, I daresay," Jane admitted grudgingly. "But I don't like it. It would be a fine thing if all the servants took it into their heads to invite their relations to come and live with them. I have instructed Henry to interview this nephew and find out what he can about him. One can never be too careful, you know."

"Now dear," protested Sir Henry Fielding rather unhappily. He was a mild, unremarkable man, prematurely balding and already possessed of a middle-aged stoop, though he was scarcely thirty-five. He seldom stood up to his far-more-formidable wife, but at least had the grace to be embarrassed by the worst of her excesses. "I'm sure it is all perfectly regular. You mustn't forget that Horsham served dear . . . er . . . Alicia's father, for a number of years."

He could not bring himself to openly defy his wife on the matter of his cousin's name, and so compromised between the two, thus ending by pleasing no one.

"Hmm. I don't mean to offend your cousin, my dear, but if you ask me, Sir William was far too lenient with his servants. They are all of them shockingly lax, and quite impertinent. Why, do you know, the other day when I had to speak to Cook about the really inferior luncheon she sent up, she had the audacity to excuse herself on the grounds that I had at the last minute asked her to put together only a very small and informal dinner for a handful of guests. Worse, she told me quite boldly that Sir William had never seen fit to complain about her meals. Really! I had to speak to her in no uncertain terms. I fear she will have to go; but then, I have always thought we should have engaged a French chef and been done with it."

For once Sir Henry looked genuinely alarmed, for he was a great trencherman. "Now, dear, you mustn't be too hasty. Mrs. Mudgely is a very good cook, and we are not in London any longer. If we begin to dismiss servants, we may very well find it difficult to replace them in such a limited district. And you know yourself how little town-bred servants like coming to the country."

"Indeed yes," put in Alessia maliciously. "In fact we were an age finding Mrs. Mudgeley. As for a French chef, Lady Evanston imported one once, to her immense regret. She was obliged to live through six months of tantrums and the increasing alienation of the other servants. And then he packed his bags and left on the night of a major dinner party."

"Yes, yes," cried Henry, quite paling at the thought of such a domestic nightmare. "You know how temperamental our own chef in London was. Mrs. Mudgely may lack his versatility, but she also lacks his moods. And I am sure I will quite happily put up with a little plain cooking for the sake of peace."

"Oh, well. I daresay it was just an idea," Jane conceded reluctantly, having herself vowed once never to employ a temperamental artist in the kitchen ever again. "But really, I will not tolerate impertinence. And as for Horsham, I hope you don't mean to persuade me we couldn't replace *him* locally if we chose?"

"I wouldn't suggest you try," said Alessia crisply. "He has been with the family for nearly thirty years, and is a great favorite, both among the other servants and in the district. Henry's right. You dismiss him, and you will soon find yourself exceedingly unpopular, I fear."

Jane looked annoyed, but obviously chose not to risk a confrontation over the issue. "Oh, well!" she said again. "I have always said I would never choose to live in such a small district. Not only are you condemned to see the same people day after day after day, but everyone knows everyone else's business. I am sure if my dear papa had not made us a present of a house in town, I should never have consented to come and live in such a provincial place."

"Now, dear!" said Henry again, glancing uncomfortably at Alessia. "You have always known that when . . . er . . . um . . . that I would inherit this house someday. And I am sure everyone has made us feel most welcome."

"Yes. Well. I hope I'm not one to complain," pointed out Jane with slight inaccuracy. "And I'm sure I've been too busy since coming here to think about being bored. Now that dear Alice is back, I shall look forward to her help again. I have had the happy notion of turning the library into a set of drawing rooms," she added with something of the air of triumph. "It really is the handsomest room in the house, and the others are quite inadequate for entertaining. Sir William was a recluse, and so can be excused, I daresay, for appropriating quite the largest apartment, but I mean to put an end to that."

Alessia experienced a rush of such anger that she was left feeling shaken. Jane had taken delight for months now in oversetting all of her previous arrangements, from the gardener's routine to the decoration of the principal rooms. Alessia had reminded herself again and again that it was only natural Jane should want to instill her own customs and personality, and tried not to take offense. But this was a deliberate declaration of war, for Jane knew how Alessia felt about the library.

It had been her father's haven for forty years, where he had done most of his work and spent his days in gentle scholarship. It housed his vast collection of books and resource materials, and Alessia never went into it without feeling his presence, even after six months. And since she had taken over his life's work and was attempting, in her humble way, to complete his translation of Dante's complete works, she still spent a great many hours in the room among old friends and shadows.

Henry, with a quick glance at her rigid face, intervened hurriedly. "Now, my love, you know . . .er . . . ah . . . Alicia uses that room still. I'm sure we shouldn't—"

"No. Jane is quite right," said Alessia, cutting him short. "It is the best room in the house, and it was remiss of me to continue to monopolize it. I will have my materials removed tomorrow."

Then she hesitated, annoyed with herself. "That is . . . I mean, of course, my father's research materials and those of his reference books I need," she amended stiltedly. "You may wish to oversee what I take."

Henry looked aghast. "No, no! It all belongs to you! I'm sure it's no use to us, and anyway, Uncle

William left it all to you expressly in his will. I wouldn't dream of—"

"Nonsense, my dear," interrupted his wife. "Alice is quite right. Your uncle did leave her his research materials—though I have always thought it a most unladylike occupation. I fear dear Alice has quite the reputation of being a bluestocking in the neighborhood! But you are your uncle's heir, and dear Mrs. Williams was telling me only the other day that his library is one of the most famous in the country. Evidently he had some quite valuable books—though I confess I know little of such matters, and find it hard to believe a mere *book* can be considered valuable. But it might be best to have the whole valued."

"I will have it done immediately," said Alessia, white with rage. "And now, if you will excuse me, I am a little tired from the journey."

Jane rose, supremely undaunted. "Certainly. We won't keep you. We only dropped by on our way to the Gracefields' for dinner. She is apallingly ill-bred, but I suppose in so limited a neighborhood one can't afford to be too choosy. I would have thought it would have occurred to you to let us know you were back, for we only found out quite by accident. Horsham also tells us you came in a hired vehicle, which gives me a very odd opinion of your friend, I must say. I would have thought that the least she could have done was to escort you safely home again."

When Alessia remained deliberately silent, she added, as if in resignation, "But then, I must inure myself to the fact that no one has any manners anymore. Which reminds me, I am giving a tea tomorrow. Only a few of the neighbors, and I am sure it will be deadly dull, but one must keep up one's end. You may oblige me by pouring out, which will leave me free to see to my duties. Clarissa is also to pass out the sandwiches and cakes."

Jane had absolutely no command over Clarissa's time and knew it, but Alessia decided to forgo this new argument. "Clarissa may naturally do as she wishes," she agreed with quiet satisfaction. "But I'm afraid I will be busy all day tomorrow. I am driving into Cheltenham to consult the library for a volume I've been needing."

Jane looked extremely annoyed, which Alessia had known she would be. Not only was she now balked of Alessia's help, but having admitted she was entertaining, she could hardly claim the need of her coachman's services, as she had frequently done in the past. It was not that she begrudged Alessia the use of the carriage, but that she was extremely jealous of her new position, and wasted no opportunity to bring Alessia's changed circumstances home to her.

After a moment she rose with majestic unconcern and took her leave, calling Henry to order when he showed an inclination to linger. "Come, dear, we must be going. After all, we mustn't intrude on dear Alice's *privacy*. I know how much it means to her."

Alessia saw them out, feeling as out-of-sorts as she usually did after one of Jane's visits. It would appear her stolen holiday had done her little good after all. She knew it was folly to allow herself to become enraged over Jane's petty slights, but she had once told Rhys the truth: no matter how often she told herself to resist, to remember why Jane was behaving that way and make allowances for her, she still found herself capable of being pierced by one of Jane's poison barbs. And she feared in the end she would grow to be exactly like her, bitter and crabbed, and unable to see any good in anyone.

And despite her renewed good intentions, Alessia took spiteful pleasure in remaining out the whole of the next day.

Horsham informed her, with a sidelong look, that his guest was settling in well enough. She knew he was far from approving of the subterfuge, but was too loyal to betray her.

"I thought it best, like, to inform Sir Henry of his presence, to stave off any gossip," he told her, again glancing obliquely at her. "But I'll confess I was a bit nervous when Sir Henry called himself last night to meet my 'nephew.' "

"Oh, dear! Did he suspect anything?"

"As to what he suspected, or didn't, I'm sure I'm not qualified to say. But I will say that your Mr. Fitzwarren seemed to take great delight in deceiving him."

"Oh, dear," she said again, more ruefully.

The coachman seemed to be choosing his words with care. "It's not my place to say anything, Miss Alessia, and you know I'm glad enough to help you. As for Mr. Fitzwarren, he seems respectable enough—overlooking a regrettable tendency to take nothing serious. To be honest, I didn't expect to hear he'd lived through that first night, for I hope never again to see anyone taken up more for dead. But I can't help wondering if you know what you've gotten yourself tangled up in."

"Then you will be pleased to know that Mr. Fitzwarren agrees with you. But I do know. And I have no intention of doing anything foolish. I promise you. Did Mr. Fitzwarren manage to convince my cousin?"

The coachman was obliged to accept her change of subject, reading it correctly as a clear warning-off. "If not, it wasn't for lack of trying," he said grudgingly. "Though I won't say he wasn't enjoying himself immensely. The missus walked in in the middle of his performance and almost dropped the tray she was carrying."

"Oh, dear," Alessia said again, amused despite herself. She guessed that Rhys had indeed been enjoying himself, and had behaved outrageously. It was lucky it had been Cousin Henry and not the sharp-eyed Jane who had called to check him out.

"Not that she didn't very soon enter into the spirit of the thing," Horsham added even more bitterly. "Womanlike, she's taken a fair shine to him, and won't hear nothing against him. You'd think he *was* her nephew, the way she already scolds him and he teases her, all on a day's acquaintance."

Alessia smiled at his obvious disapproval. "Yes, his nonsense is very appealing. But I'm glad Mrs. Horsham has taken to him. Sir Henry didn't seem to suspect anything, then?"

"No. But then, if you was to ask me, he only came on account of Lady Fielding sending him, and was a trifle put out by the whole. She's a powerful one for knowing everything that goes on in the district, she is. Meaning no disrespect, of course, and I've nothing in particular against him, but, well, he's not Sir William and never will be," he finished bluntly. "Nor can Lady Fielding hope to fill your shoes, Miss Alessia, however busy she may keep herself upsetting everything that smacks of the previous tenants. Half the servants are already up in arms and tempted to give in their notice."

Alessia was grateful for the servants' loyalty, but it had made her life very much difficult in the past months. Jane had a way of offending them, and some had taken to retaliating by informing her that "Miss Alessia always wanted it done *this* way" or "Sir William never minded about that." It was really little wonder Jane was so annoyed.

"Well, it's difficult for her, you must see that," she pointed out without much conviction. "And there are bound to be changes for everyone. It's inevitable. But no one will be served if . . . if things deteriorate to such a point as that."

"If you could hear some of the things she's said about you, Miss Alessia, I'm thinking you wouldn't be defending her. Proper harridan she is, and I make no apology for sayaing so. If I weren't so near being pensioned off, I'd give in my notice myself. But the missus quite rightly reminds me that it's Sir Henry we're working for, not her—though some would take leave to doubt it!—and that, with all the other changes, it would be disloyal in us to abandon you. And so there it is."

"Yes, I would be very unhappy if you and Mrs. Horsham were to leave," admitted Alessia, having to blink back unexpected tears. "You are one of my oldest friends. But enough of such gloomy talk. I'm happier to be back than I would have thought. It will be spring soon, and spring at the Oaks is always a beautiful time. I suspect neither of us would ever want to miss that."

But she wondered, even as she said it, if Horsham would be in the least fooled. That was the trouble with having servants who knew you too well.

11

The next morning Alessia rode her neat mare to Horsham's cottage to discover for herself how the newcomer was settling in.

It was obvious that Horsham had found the time to take him to buy new clothes, for she discovered him sitting in the weak sunshine, a straw between his teeth, looking as if he had been born there.

He rose at sight of her and threw the straw away. " 'Mornin', ma'am," he drawled in the local dialect. "Was you looking for my uncle?"

She couldn't help laughing. He wore a rough wool shirt and a leather waistcoat and serviceable breeches and looked like a handsome young rustic. She noticed, however, that he still retained his own well-made boots.

He saw her looking at them and grinned appreciatively. "We could find nothing to fit me in Wynchcombe, and I didn't feel the need to go all the way into Cheltenham. After all, I have been a batman, so possibly I inherited my boots from my master. In point of fact I had them made in Spain, and I confess would be loath to part with them. Have you really come to see Horsham?"

"Yes, ostensibly to discuss my mare. But in reality to see how you're settling in. Come around back where no one can see us."

He obligingly touched his forelock and grinned at her, and she laughed again and led the way around the house.

He followed more slowly, but the average

observer would not guess that he had so recently been near death. He walked with a certain stiffness, and his right arm still rested in its sling, but little else betrayed him.

He intercepted her look and seemed to read her thoughts, as he so often did, for he said, "Yes, I am more or less fully recovered. Though we set it about that I had recently been injured, and that was what had driven me to look up my long-lost uncle. Mrs. Horsham thought it would be less of a risk."

"Yes, Horsham said she had taken you under her wing," Alessia freed her knee from the horn and gathered up her skirts, ignoring his offer of help to slip neatly to the ground. "Thank you, but you are not *that* much recovered. At any rate, I am used to riding alone. Are they making you comfortable?" She tied the mare's reins loosely to a convenient tree and strolled toward an attractive copse.

"Very. I fear Mrs. Horsham is mothering me already. Did Horsham tell you we received a visit from your cousin?"

"Henry? Yes. I'm afraid Jane sent him. Horsham said he seemed rather embarrassed. And that you enjoyed making him look a fool," she added sternly, trying to keep her amusement from showing.

"It was totally unnecessary, believe me! He did that without any of my help."

She went to seat herself on an overturned log, also enjoying the mild sunshine after so many days of bad weather. "Henry's not so bad, really. He was a good-enough companion as a youth, when we used to play together. It's just that his will has never been strong, and Jane tends to dominate him."

He grinned at her. "Poor fellow. I begin to see why you hated to come back so much. Mrs. Horsham is quite one of your most devoted followers, in case you didn't know it. I have already heard a great deal about the new Sir Henry and Lady Fielding. It seems they are not universally popular."

She made a face. "No. And I'm grateful, but people like Mrs. Horsham won't see that they're only making things worse. In Jane's defense—which I admit I am not often willing to give her—it can't be easy to come in as the outsider. But perhaps you can see now why I said it would have been better had I left the district immediately."

"Why the devil should you let the unpleasant Jane drive you away from your home?" he demanded.

"Because it isn't my home any longer. And I have come to realize I would be far happier away from here, with all its memories. I have also come to realize that I am a great deal more mean-spirited and petty than I had ever wanted to believe myself. Try as I might, to see Jane turning all the rooms upside down and instituting all her own routines and customs in place of my own fills me with rage. As for poor Henry usurping Papa's role—"

Then she shook off such gloomy thoughts. "But I didn't come to talk of that. I came, instead, to tell you that I exceeded my authority and did some research yesterday. And what I found out is most interesting, I think."

When he looked puzzled, she quietly told him of her previous day's activities. "I had Horsham drive me over to Crickfield yesterday, just to see what I could discover. And before you can say anything, it was all perfectly safe, for I have often driven that way."

He had instantly frowned, and she added quickly, "And don't scowl so at me. I took care to be extremely discreet. I just happened to stop at a cottage near your home to ask for a drink of water. As I had hoped, it turned out to be one of your father's tenants, and his wife was most kind. She insisted upon my coming in and taking tea with her; and what is much more to the point, was an extremely gossipy old soul. And as Crickfield is the largest house in the neighborhood, she was remarkably familiar with what is happening there."

"Good God! You have been busy. Very well. What did you manage to find out by this amazing subterfuge?"

"Nothing immediately to the point, regrettably," she admitted. "Except that you are still remembered and spoken of, and the neighborhood seems as shocked as you were by your father's change of will. Many, of course, blame you for abandoning your responsibilities, but Mrs. Inching did say in your defense that your father was known to be a 'powerful hard man.' He was liked in the district for struggling so long to keep up the estate, but his extreme pride was well-known. You didn't tell me that one of your uncles was the Earl of Petworth, by the way."

His lean face lightened into a grin. "Ah, a foolish oversight on my part! That would undoubtedly have made me instantly acceptable to you, for a more pompous, priggish slowtop than my uncle Francis I've yet to meet. He was also, in a nutshell, the crux of most of the quarrels between my father and myself. You see, my father could never forgive himself for having been born a younger son, and spent his life trying to build up a heritage worthy of the one he had missed by so slight a margin. Unfortunately, I found such religious allegiance to the Fitzwarren name both foolish and wearing. Which was undoubtedly what in the end led to my disinheritance. I couldn't be trusted, you see, to carry on the holy crusade."

"And your uncle Walter can be?" she asked curiously.

"I don't know. I had thought that that particular sickness was limited to my father, but to tell the truth, I didn't know my Uncle Walter all that well. He's a younger son too, of course, and even more pompous and stiff-rumped than my father, if possible. We didn't see much of each other. He has a property near Abingdon, and though my cousin Owen was used to spend his summers with us, my uncle himself seldom came. I never thought he and my father got on that well, though it was all very civilized. *Family,* you see, meant everything, and so one didn't admit that one didn't like one's own brothers."

"Well, if so, the rift seems to have been healed," she remarked. "At least where your Uncle Walter is concerned. According to Mrs. Inching, both your uncle and cousin came to live with your father the last year of his life. Making sure of your disinheritance, do you suppose?"

He did look rather startled at that. "Are you certain? My uncle's property was always far more prosperous than Crickfield. I wouldn't have thought he would abandon it to come and nurse a brother he had never been all that close to."

"Be that as it may, they both left it to make their home with your father that last year—a fact a few in the district found significant in light of the subsequent will your father left, again according to Mrs. Inching. But the general view seems to be that it was more an act of charity than avarice. If Crickfield has suddenly increased dramatically in value, I'm sorry to say the neighborhood doesn't know of it."

He was still frowning slightly, but he looked up

at that. "I can believe that, at least. But I will admit I'm surprised by the others. Particularly in my cousin's case. Owen used to make as much fun of Crickfield and my father's obsession as I did."

"Well, he seems now to be the fair-haired boy in the neighborhood. Your uncle Walter is not much liked yet, for he holds himself extremely high in the instep, according to the reliable Mrs. Inching. But Owen has taken the time to cultivate the locals. Mrs. Inching, at least, will be glad when he becomes the master in his father's place."

"Well, he's welcome to it, for all of me," Rhys said lightly, though there remained a faint frown in his eyes. "Your Mrs. Inching seems to have been a veritable gold mine. She's new since my time, for I don't remember her. But then, I daresay a lot of other things have changed as well."

"More than you know," agreed Alessia dryly. "Which brings me to the most interesting part of my discoveries. Mrs. Inching says that within the last year most of the old servants have been pensioned off. She seems to think it natural enough, for they were getting on in years; but I must confess I find it highly suspicious on top of everything else."

But at that he merely grinned. "You are determined to make a mystery of this, aren't you? I could give you a dozen perfectly logical explanations for everything you've told me. But it would be unkind in me to spoil your fun."

"Well, I will admit I enjoyed myself yesterday. But I am far from taking it as lightly as you do, you know. The fact remains that someone did try to kill you, and later came back to make sure of his handiwork."

"Oh, I don't take it at all lightly," he protested. "My sore ribs serve to remind me of just exactly how serious it is. And I am more than impressed and flattered by your initiative—though we will speak of that again later! But I must confess I still find it all strangely hard to believe. We still stick at the motive for doing me in so brutally, you know. Even if my uncle does share fully in my father's obsessive pride, Crickfield is hardly worth doing murder to obtain."

"Maybe not, but I intend to find out. In her ramblings Mrs. Inching also disclosed the valuable information that Crickfield is noted locally for its library. I can easily use that to obtain an entry, for my father was well-known in the district, you know."

There was a deep, appreciative twinkle in his eyes, but he said bluntly, "No, you are to keep out of it. I won't have you risking any more danger than you already have."

"Pooh! I'm in no danger. And at any rate, if you are as convinced as you say of your uncle's innocence, there can be no harm in my proving it. Nor, might I point out, can you stop me. I have had my fill of people trying to run my life."

He saw she was serious, and wisely tried another tack. "What, are you still hoping to find a lost Titian or an early Gutenberg Bible? Have you given up on the possibility of the maze with a treasure in stolen jewels buried at the center of it?"

"You can make as much fun as you like, but I am convinced there must be something behind it. And I should find it easy enough to contrive to be left alone in the library. In fact I intend to talk so long and boringly on my father's specialty that your uncle will be eager to abandon me. *And* if I time my arrival carefully, he will even be obliged to invite me to lunch, don't you think? I have discovered a curiosity in myself to get to know Lord Walter Fitzwarren."

This time he did laugh. "You should have no trouble at all—especially if my cousin Owen is there. He always had an eye for a pretty face."

"Then I shall have to hope he is," she said serenely. "But now that I come to think about it, I shall have to take care not to seem too boring, for I don't want to scare your uncle off completely. And if he does invite me to share his lunch, I should think it will be easy enough to obtain a tour of the entire house, don't you?"

"Extremely easy. I only wish I might be a fly on the wall! But what do you hope to gain by all this effort?"

"Well, I don't like to boast, but my eyes are extremely sharp, you know. If there is some undiscovered treasure in the house, I will back myself to find it. My somewhat unusual background must be good for something."

He was still smiling lazily at her, enjoying her enthusiasm and the way her cheeks pinkened when she was excited. "A very good deal, I am beginning to discover. But though I don't mean to be depressingly practical, the chances are extremely high that if such a treasure existed, my uncle would have long since sold it—or at least hidden it. Have you thought of that?"

"Yes, but I don't think he can have," she pointed out confidently. "As a matter of fact, I've given it a lot of thought, and in the first place, it would look far too suspicious if he unexpectedly inherited the property over your head and then turned up an unknown and highly valuable asset. And if he had already sold it, why would he need to worry about removing you?"

"Again, I hesitate to dampen your enthusiasm, but I confess I can think of any number of reasons.

I might notice the missing painting—or sculpture or whatever—and ask about it. And it stands to reason I might come to learn of the sale. As you say, that might indeed rouse my suspicions, if they had not been aroused already."

"Then you do consider it a possibility!" she cried triumphantly.

He frowned, wondering if he did. Despite her obvious conviction, he still found it difficult to believe his uncle could have been responsible for the attack on him. That was, admittedly, due more to the lack of motive than any deep-seated belief that his uncle was incapable of such an act, but it amounted to the same thing.

But at the same time, he found he didn't have the heart to completely dampen her enjoyment of her own theory. He had heard quite enough from his kindly hostess by then to know that Alessia got little enough pleasure out of life these days. If she were enjoying herself, he saw no harm in allowing her to continue a little longer. Even if all her wild imaginings should prove to be true, against every probability, his uncle had no reason to connect her with him, of course. And she was right that he could hardly stop her if she chose to play sleuth against his wishes.

For himself, he was growing more and more convinced that the shooting had been a simple case of mistaken identity. His famous luck had indeed deserted him and he had had the simple misfortune of being in the wrong place at the wrong time. With each passing day it seemed to become more and more unreal to him, as if it had happened in another life. Only his sore ribs and the by now heartily despised sling remained to remind him that it had really happened.

It was a complacency he would shortly have reason to regret, but at the time he saw no possible danger in allowing her to continue her harmless games a little longer.

12

As she had boasted, Alessia found it surprisingly easy to gain admittance to Crickfield.

Judging that if indeed he had something to hide, it would be wiser not to give Lord Walter Fitzwarren a chance to put her off, she decided against writing to him and requesting an appointment. Consequently, with a boldness that inwardly appalled her, she drove up to the house and handed her visiting card to the neat footman who opened the door to her.

She didn't find Crickfield as depressing as Rhys had made it out to be. It was both unmistakably of the William-and-Mary era, and larger than she had expected. It also gave an impression of solidity and ancient family lineage that Rhys's father, Edward Fitzwarren, seemed to have sought all his life. It could not compare with Newton Abbey, the principal seat of the Earl of Petworth, of course. But it was a handsome old house.

But from her own experience she could also see that without a substantial income to support it, it could easily become an expensive millstone round its owner's neck. And as if to bear this out, her experienced eye picked out the subtle signs of age and deterioration that would be extremely expensive to arrest.

Lord Edward Fitzwarren seemed to have kept up the facade very well, but if Rhys was to be believed, the cost had already begun depleting his private fortune years ago. The stubborn pride that would sacrifice everything to a house, and one not even of long standing in the family, was foreign to her. But she had little trouble believing there were men like that Her cousin Henry was so proud of being Sir Henry Fielding of the Oaks that she thought he would give up almost anything before he would give that up. To a younger son in a powerful family, being Fitzwarren of Crickfield, a venerable and respected property, must have meant everything to him.

She found that Lord Walter Fitzwarren bore little resemblance to his black-sheep nephew. At first glance he certainly didn't look like a murderer either—but since she had no idea what a murderer looked like, she refused to allow that to weigh with her.

He brushed aside her apologies for having arrived without warning, assured her he was only too happy to have the library put to good use, and confessed that he himself was no scholar. But he did it all in a bored way that conveyed no particular warmth or charm.

She had been counting on his ignorance, however, and so talked impressively of folios and the first reference to Dante by Chaucer, and an earlier, incomplete translation by one Jonathan Richardson, an unknown artist.

Lord Walter maintained a look of polite interest on his face, but soon found an excuse to conduct her to the library and leave her.

Alessia smiled to herself at her success so far, and began her search.

Her task might appear, to the uninitiated, to be exceedingly daunting, but she had chosen the library first because it was her particular area of expertise. It was also the one where a valuable collection was most likely to remain unnoticed by careless and unscholarly owners.

But though she exhausted herself climbing to the highest shelves and pulling out dusty volumes that had lain unopened for centuries, she found nothing of particular value. She found one or two that her father would have enjoyed, but they were not intrinsically valuable. And she found a quarto Shakespeare that was interesting, if not particularly rare, and a number of lesser first editions.

She also nearly gave herself away once, for she was on the library steps reaching for an elusive volume just out of reach on the top shelf when a maid came in to invite her to take lunch with his lordship.

Alessia straightened so rapidly she almost overbalanced, and knew that her face was betrayingly red. The maid indeed looked surprised to see his lordship's guest so strenuously engaged, but curtsied politely and delivered her message.

Alessia made herself take a deep breath and then answer naturally. She feared her dress was dusty and her hair coming down in the back, for she had had little time and a large library to search. But she calmly descended the steps, dusting her skirts as she came. "I'm afraid some of the books are dreadfully dusty. But then, I know from my own experience that such large libraries are almost impossible to keep clean. I thought I saw a particularly rare translation of Virgil in that corner, but it appears I was mistaken."

As she had expected, the maid looked even more bewildered, but bobbed another curtsy. "Yes, miss. His lordship is not particularly scholarly, nor was his brother before him, so no one comes in here much. If you don't mind, miss, his lordship is waiting in the dining room."

"Very well. Tell his lordship I will join him as soon as I have had a chance to freshen up. And you really should have a thorough cleaning in here one day. Books not dusted and aired are quickly ruined, you know," Alessia said sternly, keeping to her role.

"Yes, miss."

The maid led her to an empty bedroom on the second floor, where water and towels had been laid out for her use, and waited while Alessia washed her hands and tidied her hair. Alessia was frustrated, for she thus had no time to do anything more than look quickly around her before she was escorted down again to the dining room.

She found her host there before her. He rose and bowed at her entrance, then conducted her to a seat with courtly courtesy, and made polite conversation throughout the meal. But again no warmth animated him. Except for the fact she was extremely loath to give up her pet theory, she would have thought Lord Walter Fitzwarren far too cold and passionless a creature ever to order murder done.

Certainly, in the face of his well-bred indifference, she found her self-assigned role of aggressive scholarship somewhat wearing to maintain. He asked politely after her research without listening to her answer, but gave no hint that she was anything more threatening than a slightly tedious nuisance. He even insisted that she must come again if she didn't finish her work, and that he was delighted to have the library put to such good use.

Alessia was baffled, for it did seem as if he had nothing to hide. But also for the first time she began to understand a little of what Rhys must have been up against as a boy. If the older brother had been anything like the younger, pride was clearly the greatest part of their makeup. Lord Walter behaved politely to her because to do anything else would have been beneath him, not out of any deference to her. *Noblesse oblige* indeed!

Indeed, as lunch progressed she found herself disliking her host more and more. Whether that made him a murderer, she had no idea, but she was rapidly coming to believe anyone so coldly dispassionate was capable of anything.

In the end she couldn't resist an attempt to prick him out of the well-bred air of polite boredom. "But I understand you have just come into this property, Lord Walter," she said provocatively.

But he betrayed no reluctance at the change in topic. "Yes, from my brother."

"He had no sons himself, then?"

He politely offered her a peach and began peeling it for her, his well-kept hand never faltering. "Yes, one. They quarreled years ago, and he chose not to leave his property to him," he answered indifferently, quartering the peach and putting it on a plate before handing it to her. "It was not entailed, so he was free to do as he wished with it."

"Yes, but that seems so cruel!" she insisted, looking, she hoped, sufficiently fatuous. "I mean, Papa's greatest regret was that he had no son to leave his property to. There is nothing like family, I always say."

He was now calmly peeling a peach for himself. "But then, Sir William had you to carry on his life's work," he remarked. The words might have been gallant had the cold tone not robbed them of anything remotely personal. "I'm afraid my nephew did nothing but disappoint his father."

"Oh, do tell me about it!" She leaned her chin on her hand and regarded him beguilingly. Since she had already made a fool of herself, she decided she might as well complete the job. "I love family scandals, don't you? Oh, dear! That sounds terribly naughty of me, but you must admit they are almost always far more fascinating than any novel. Don't you agree?"

"Since this scandal involved my family, I think I may be forgiven for not finding it particularly fascinating," he returned dryly. "But since my nephew also made absolutely no attempt to keep his excesses a secret, anyone in the district can tell you of them. I fear he was a young care-for-nobody who cost my poor brother a fortune from first to last. When my brother finally determined to put an end to it, they quarreled violently for the last time and my nephew fled abroad. He has not been heard from since."

And that's one for you, she thought crudely. Given his earlier reticence, she though he seemed a little too eager to get his side of the story out. "You mean, he didn't even come back after his father's death?" she asked in a shocked voice. "But then, perhaps he hasn't heard of it yet."

"He has almost certainly heard of it. May I offer you a little more coffee? My brother's solicitor wrote to him, apprising him of the fact, you know. We have heard nothing in return."

She decided to needle him a little more. "But how did the solicitor know where to write if you haven't heard from him since he left?" she asked innocently.

She thought his cold eyes rested on her for an instant, but he said merely, in the indifferent voice she was coming to know well, "He had, naturally, written to the solicitor from time to time, requesting more money. I believe that is how the solicitor knew where to find him."

"Oh, then your brother didn't quite cut him off without a penny? I'm so glad. It seems so . . . so unrelenting, somehow."

"I believe my nephew had a small income of his own, from his mother's side of the family," he said, sounding bored now with the topic. She feared she had overplayed her hand, and he would shortly make an excuse to leave her. But he seemed to wrestle with himself about something for a moment, then added more tolerantly, "At any rate, my son feels as you do, and has always had a soft spot for his cousin. Should my nephew return, he will always find a home here, even though his father chose not to leave it to him. Now, if you are quite finished, I fear I have an unavoidable appointment this afternoon and must leave you. I hope we may do this again sometime. It has been delightful."

Why don't I believe that? she thought cynically as she obediently rose. "Yes, of course! I have taken up far too much of your valuable time already," she said warmly, still managing to inject a vague disappointment in her tone. Really, she had never known she had such a flair for acting. "It's just that . . . Oh, dear, after all your kindness, I don't know how to ask you."

She could see that he was unmoved by her pretty show of confusion, but he was too well-bred to ignore such an obvious hint. "Was there something else I could do for you, Miss Fielding?" he asked, betraying nothing but a rather weary resignation.

But then, she was forced to acknowledge that he had good reason. Indeed, nothing he had done that morning could be considered out of character for a well-bred gentleman confronted with an unwanted and rather pushing guest.

But still, for some reason she was more convinced than ever that he was behind the mysterious attack on his nephew. Nothing he had said or done might have been suspicious, but he had broken his polite reticence only on the subject of his nephew. It seemed to her that despite all his coolness he had been oddly eager to put forward an unimpeachable explanation for his brother's extraordinary will. A ne-er-do-well nephew, conveniently absent—or dead!—and thus unable to defend himself, could be made to appear the author of his own fate, and thus unworthy of anyone's sympathy or concern.

If Lord Walter Fitzwarren had conspired to have his nephew disinherited, and then to murder him, he would be exceedingly anxious to avoid any hint of mystery or speculation. And a chattering fool such as Alessia had shown herself to be that morning might be relied upon to spread the tale he had told her far and wide, which was undoubtedly what he was counting on.

So she made herself say, as if reluctantly, "Oh, nothing! Really, you have been far too kind already. It's just that one of my passions happens to be William-and-Mary architecture, and I really don't think I've seen quite such an impressive example before. I was hoping I could see through it—but of course, if you have an appointment, I wouldn't dream of intruding. Perhaps another time. I fear I have been dreadfully rude and presumptuous already."

In the face of that, he could do nothing else but say politely, "Of course. I fear I must deny myself the pleasure of escorting you, but you must by all means see it, though I fear you'll find it somewhat neglected. My brother, you know, had already discovered that his income was insufficient to keep it. Indeed, I'm beginning to suspect anyone's would be. I fear I can't share your passion—and indeed my brother's—for such outmoded grandeur. I far prefer my own estates, less impressive I'll grant you, but far more comfortable and productive."

Ah, he did that very well, she acknowledged, but still it didn't ring quite true. Everything he said was undoubtedly true, but a man of his pride and breeding would never discuss such intimate financial details with a total stranger, least of all a woman, and one of her demonstrated inquisitiveness.

She made herself say foolishly, "Oh, don't you mean to keep it, then? What a shame!"

Once again he seemed to hesitate. Then he shrugged. "I really haven't decided yet. And now, I fear I really must leave you. I have rung for a maid to show you through the house. I can only repeat that it has all been quite delightful and I hope you will return whenever you are in the district. I will leave instructions to admit you even if I'm not here."

And that's one for me, she thought ruefully. Surely if he had something to hide he wouldn't invite her to return whenever she chose.

Rhys's skepticism began to return to haunt her, and it was difficult after that to embark on the tour of the house with her previous enthusiasm.

Only the fact that she had never met anyone she liked less kept her going. Insufferable pride, of course, was not murder. But she shivered a little in the warm hallway, the memory of those cold eyes still on her, and had little trouble believing Lord Walter Fitzwarren capable of anything.

In the estate office, in the meantime, Lord Walter stood for a moment, his eyes questioning and his expression far from pleasant. Then he shook the mood off and went to keep his appointment.

13

Alessia was not surprised that the tour through the house proved disappointing.

She poked and pried unforgivably, using her supposed expert knowledge to excuse her peering at paintings in dark corners and picking up and inspecting everything that might possibly be valuable. But though she blushed at her own brazen behavior, she found nothing even remotely likely to have prompted an attempt at murder.

The furnishings were all heavy and ornate, and the paintings and ornaments tended to be likewise. She supposed it was all valuable enough, but hardly worth a fortune. Nor did she find any lost Van Dycks or Rubenses.

She did find a portrait of a young Rhys, obviously with his cousin, that she stood before for some time, for once having no need to feign interest. Both looked about twenty and touchingly carefree. Rhys was standing with his hand on the shoulder of his cousin, who was seated. His other hand held a book, as if he had just looked up from his reading. It was an excellent portrait that seemed to have caught the essence of both. There was mischief in Rhys's eyes, and already that hint of charming impenetrability that was so much a part of him now. His cousin looked far more sober and thoughtful.

She looked at the image of Owen almost as long. He was admittedly graver, but at least at that age betrayed none of his father's cold formality. She thought him less appealing than Rhys, but he looked even-tempered and reliable, as befitted the responsible cousin who stayed home.

They had reputedly been good friends as boys. She wondered if Owen knew of his father's actions, and what he thought of his questionable new inheritance.

By dint of gossiping shamelessly with the maid she was able to learn a few things of possible interest. It seemed Betty had not been employed there when the young master was still around, but she had seen him in the village, of course. He had been well-liked, for he wasn't a bit unapproachable.

Aye, everyone had been surprised when the house had gone to Lord Walter, for old Lord Edward was known to be so proud, no one had believed he would actually disinherit his own son. But then Mr. Rhys had run off, hadn't he, and nothing more had ever been heard from him. He might even be dead, for all they knew. And it wasn't for the likes of her to question.

Yes, Lord Walter was well-enough-received, though his son, Mr. Owen, was the better-liked. It was said he and Mr. Rhys had been fond of each other, and he had been heard to say openly in the village once or twice that he was sorry things had come to such a pass.

Were there any of the old servants still around in the district? Yes, there was old Granny Lewisham, what had been nurse to the young master, and lived in Pershore with her daughter. She was getting on in years, but still spry enough, for Betty had seen her only last fall.

Committing the name to memory, and feeling that she had outlasted even her thin excuses, Alessia thanked the girl, slipped her a douceur, and took her leave, her thoughts exceedingly busy.

The result of all this thought was that on the return home she instructed Horsham to make a detour, and paid a visit on Granny Lewisham.

As Betty had reported, she proved to be a spry, comfortably rounded dame of uncertain years, engaged when Alessia arrived in rolling out a pie crust. She answered the door herself, her arms liberally sprinkled with flour, and explained at length that her daughter was away, tending to her youngest's first confinement, and that was why she herself was seeing to her son-in-law's supper.

Alessia had wondered what excuse she could give for calling on the old woman, but it soon became clear she needed none. Mrs. Lewisham was glad enough for the company, and quite willing to talk about anything and everything.

She begged to be allowed to finish the pie, since Joe was always that hungry when he came in from the fields. A good man was Joe, not like some she could name. Her Mary had never had any cause to regret having married him. Nor had he made any complaint when his mother-in-law had come to live with him, as many a man would.

"Not that I contemplated ever retiring, you understand," she ended, rolling out her pastry with surprising vigor. "I can tend a baby now as well as ever I could, and I must admit I'd hoped to dandle Mr. Rhys's infants on my knee the same as I did him. But there, it just goes to show one never knows, doesn't it?"

She sighed, looking briefly sad, then brushed back her hair with a floury hand and resumed her vigorous assault on the dough. "Nor it don't do no good to repine, is what I always say. I'm happy enough here, and I've no objection to taking it easy in my old age. Lord Walter was generous enough, I will give him that. As for Master Rhys, who knows where he is or even if he's alive, poor boy?"

"Lord Walter told me he hadn't been heard from since he left," Alessia said curiously.

The nurse looked up, plainly surprised. "Oh, no! No, indeed," she said positively. "I know myself that isn't right, for Lord Edward—Master Rhys's father, you know—was used to tell me whenever he got a letter from him. There wasn't many, and considering some of the outlandish places they came from, I'm sure it was little wonder. But Lord Edward, for all his gruffness, was glad enough to get them, that I will say."

"Were you surprised, then, that he left everything to his brother?"

Mrs. Lewisham hesitated. "Well, I was, and that's a fact," she conceded. "His lordship had a bitter temper—both of 'em had, if it comes to that—and they'd quarreled for as long as I can remember. But Master Rhys, at least, was so sunny-tempered it seldom lasted long with him. Lord Edward was not so easy, but for all his pride, no father was fonder of his son than what he was, that I'll always maintain. And they wrote to each other now and then, like I told you. I thought the quarrel had long ago blown over. But I daresay his lordship resented Master Rhys continuing to stay away, and chose that way to get back at him. Powerful stiff-necked he was, and not one to take a slight lying down. Aye, that must have been it," she ended comfortably, and went back to her work.

"And of course he must have been very fond of his brother. I understand Lord Walter came to stay with him the last year of his life, neglecting his own estates."

"Aye, there was that too. Though I wouldn't have said . . . But then, neither of 'em was ever one to wear his heart on his sleeve, that I will say. And to give him his due, Lord Walter took good care of his brother that last year. He was ill most of it, you see, and not the most pleasant of patients. I should know, for many was the time I took him his medicine or sat through the night with him, though it was precious little appreciation I ever got for it—or wanted."

"Did he never think of sending for his son in that last year?"

Again Nurse Lewisham stopped what she was going. "Now, it's funny you should ask that," she said. "I suggested it to him once, as a matter of fact. He flew out at me, and swore something proper, as was his way, saying if his son didn't care enough to come and see how he did, then he didn't want him near him. But I suspected it was just bluster. And later I stumbled upon a letter he'd written to Master Rhys in Greece, where he was at the time, asking him to return."

Alessia was suddenly alert. "Did he send it, do you know?" she asked quickly.

"No, miss, that I don't. I guess he can't have, for Master Rhys never came, though I don't know what became of it. And his brother, to do him credit, put up with his crotchets, and was as patient as you could wish with him. I'm not one to let my feelings blind me to another's good qualities, that I will say."

"Then you don't like Lord Walter?" Alessia asked bluntly.

" 'Tisn't my place to like him or dislike him," said the nurse serenely. "But he's a cold one, that I'll grant you. Fortunately his son's not like him, for him and Master Rhys used to be great friends, you know. And he's become mighty popular locally of late. I think most will be glad when the son inherits, if we're to be denied having Master Rhys at the big house."

The nurse deftly placed her pastry in the pan, shaped and filled it, and slipped it into the oven. "Aye, that will go down nice with Joe's dinner, if I do say so myself," she pronounced complacently. "A proper one for his pudding, he is. I tell my daughter she spoils him, but then, a little spoiling never hurt anyone, I always say."

"No, indeed. It looks wonderful," Alessia said truthfully. "Tell me, Mrs. Lewisham, was there anything unusual that happened that last year of Lord Edward's life? The answer could be very important."

The nurse looked surprised, but thankfully asked no awkward questions, and obligingly seemed to cast her mind back in time. She rocked on her heels a little, her hands tucked at her waist and her face thoughtful. Then abruptly her eyes widened. "Now that you mention it, there *was* something. It's curious, for I hadn't given it a thought up until this minute, what with everything else that happened. But I thought it was odd at the time, I will confess. Lord Edward, you understand, had grown increasingly irritable them last years, and wouldn't have strangers in the house. But then, a few months before he died, at Lord Walter's insistence, he did have a stranger in to stay. He was very much against it, though, for I heard them arguing over it. Lord Edward declared he wouldn't have anyone in the house, no matter who he was, and began to get all excited, as he tended to do. I couldn't hear what Lord Walter said in return, but in the end he must have talked him round, for the man came to stay not a week later."

"Was it an old friend of Lord Edward's?"

"No, indeed! That's what made it so curious. His lordship refused even to see him, nor he wasn't a real gentleman, if you take my meaning. Quite common I thought him, though he seemed nice enough, to give him his due. He stayed for almost a week, and did nothing but tramp around the grounds. You might not know it, but all the farms were sold off long ago. All that's left of the original estate is some mountainous property that's no good to anyone. It was that he was tramping over, for he'd come in tired and muddy every night. Aye, and with his pockets filled with nasty rocks, for Mrs. Purdy, the housekeeper that was then, was always complaining about it."

"Rocks?" queried Alessia, feeling a strange excitement welling up in her. "Can you remember what kind of rocks?"

"Well, now, one rock is the same as another to me, dear. Master Rhys was always dirtying his pockets with 'em as a little boy, but that's only natural at that age. I never bothered to study any of 'em, just chucked 'em away. But it's different in a grown man. It fair had both of us puzzled, I will admit. Oh, here's Joe! I'm sorry, miss, for I've enjoyed our little chat, but Joe will be wanting his supper now. Powerful set on his food is my daughter's husband."

Joe indeed stamped in then, looking somewhat taken aback at his mother-in-law's elegant visitor. He touched his hat civilly enough, then stood waiting awkwardly, plainly ill-at-ease, and Alessia had no choice but to take her leave.

She thanked the talkative little nurse for her help, promised to call again when she was in the neighborhood, and stepped out of the low cottage cursing Joe's timing. He could not have chosen a worse moment to return for his supper, for she had the feeling she was getting close to something important—perhaps the all-importnt motive that Rhys insisted upon.

But there was nothing to do but take her leave, at the moment no nearer a solution than before. The man with the rocks might mean anything, or nothing. It was certainly all very frustrating.

Rhys seemed amused at Alessia's failure to discover anything of value in his old home. "I feared you would be disappointed. The very fact my uncle let you poke your nose around indicates he has nothing to hide. You look ravishing, by the way. I hope my uncle was properly appreciative?"

In honor of the occasion she had broken out a new lavender silk gown, deciding it was more than time she converted to half-mourning. She had decided, in a discontented session before her mirror, that Rhys was right. Black made her look haggish and she was sick to death of it.

"Thank you, but don't try to distract me," she retorted. "I must confess I didn't take to your uncle very much."

He grinned. "What, did he treat you to the long-line-of-earl's-at-his-back civility? He and my father both did it very well, I must confess."

"Yes, but it was more than that. He might be excused for being short with me, for I will admit I behaved with appalling vulgarity. Really, I never knew I was such an actress before. I must have more of my mo . . ."

There her smile abruptly faded and she looked away for a moment, her cheeks betrayingly hot. "N-never mind," she finished hurriedly at last, striving to regain her composure. "The point is, as proud as Lord Walter obviously is, he tolerated my rude questions far too well. I was exceedingly impertinent, you know, and asked him all sorts of personal questions. But instead of snubbing me, as I fully expected him to do, he seemed to be at some pains to establish his side of the story. And he lied to me point-blank on several issues. He told me you had never been heard of since you left six years ago, for instance."

He was still looking highly amused. "Well, that is admittedly suspicious, but hardly condemns him out of hand."

"He also told me you had been an extremely expensive young man, and that is why you quarreled with your father that last time."

Rhys snorted at last. "I wish I might have been. I had the will, but not the means. I was admittedly a worthless-enough young fool, but the major reason we usually quarreled was that my father kept me on such a short rein. Everything went to that damn mausoleum of his. He was obsessed by the subject. His income not being what he considered sufficient to the task, he had long since begun to tap into his principal, and would have made inroads on the income left me from my mother if it had been possible. If he had a thousand guineas to leave in his will, I'd be surprised."

"Yes, I could see the results," she admitted thoughtfully. "Nothing looked too obviously shabby, but there were a good many signs of a general decline. I found it a handsome-enough house, but I must confess I am beginning to doubt Crickfield itself can possibly be the motive—unless he really is as obsessed as your father on the subject."

"Handsome and exceedingly uncomfortable. What few guests my father would ever tolerate used to complain incessantly of the drafty rooms and endless passages. Myself, I grew up on cold meals and lukewarm shaving water, so I was used to it. And at least it prepared me for some of the primitive conditions I was to meet later on my travels, though I doubt my father would have been gratified to hear it. At any rate, bad as it was, it was far better than Newton Abbey, my father's boyhood home, so I daresay he never even noticed its many inconveniences."

But that succeeded in reminding her of the one useful piece of information she had managed to uncover, and her eyes began to dance. "Which reminds me, I paid a visit to your old nurse as well. The maid told me she still lived in the neighborhood."

He looked startled. "Good God! How is she?"

"Very well. She was pensioned off with the rest of the older servants, and seemed to regret she would never be able to dandle your infants on her knees, but she seems happy with her daughter and son-in-law."

He grinned appreciatively. "Good old Lewie. She always was an optimist. I fear she won't live long enough to dandle any infants of mine. But I was always fond of her."

"And she you. She confirmed, by the way, that your father had gotten over the last quarrel between you, for he used to share the contents of your letters with her. She was puzzled by his abrupt *volte-face* in his will, but since the will seemed to be valid, shrugged off her doubts. She also told me that Lord Edward and his brother were far from being on amicable terms the last year of your father's life, *and* that she once saw a letter your father was writing to you in Greece during his last illness, asking you to return," she added with satisfaction.

He frowned and then shrugged. "I never received it, but then, the mails there were unreliable, to say the least. It may have gotten lost."

"Or it may have been intercepted! It would have

been inconvenient to have you turn up at that time, to put the lie to the story that the breach between you had never been healed."

"You are determined to lay the blame on my uncle, aren't you?" He grinned.

"I am only determined to find out the truth. But to get back to my story, there *was* one occurrence in that last year that Mrs. Lewisham found puzzling. And you needn't continue to grin like that," she said indignantly. "I am aware you think it all nonsense, but now that I have met your uncle, I am more convinced I'm right than ever."

"Very well," he said, dutifully schooling his expression. "What was this mysterious occurrence?"

"I've half a mind not to tell you, only it's so curious I can't keep it to myself," she grumbled. "Mrs. Lewisham also mentioned that your father hated visitors—especially near the end. But despite that, he did have a mysterious visitor in the last year, one imported by Lord Walter and who caused Lord Edward to protest violently and refuse even to see him."

"Well, at the risk of offending you again, I must point out there's nothing so remarkable in that," he said mildly. "If my uncle were to have any visitors, it would have had to be over my father's violent objections—and he almost certainly would have refused to see them himself."

"Yes, but this one spent his time tramping about the property on mysterious errands, and according to Mrs. Lewisham, he used to return with his pockets filled with dirty rocks." She produced her trump card triumphantly, and watched his face expectantly for his reaction.

For once she was not disappointed. His brows drew together, and he whistled a little, obviously surprised. "Well, that does sound curious, I'll admit, though I daresay there might be any of a dozen plausable explanations for it. Perhaps he just liked to collect rocks. I know I used to when I was a boy."

"So Mrs. Lewisham informed me. But still, admit it, you were slightly shaken! Don't try to deny it."

"I'll admit it. Shaken, but not bowed. It's interesting, but it still proves nothing."

"I am beginning to think you are equally determined to be obtuse! Unfortunately, Mrs. Lewisham couldn't remember what kind they were, and admitted she wouldn't know one rock from another. She started to tell me something else, but then her son-in-law came in for his dinner, and she was prevented, which was most annoying. I wonder what it was," she mused aloud.

He grimaced. "I'm beginning to dread the answer. This whole thing has gotten out of hand."

"Then you do think there's something mysterious about it!" She pounced on the admission.

"I don't know. I will confess only to wishing I'd never allowed you to get involved. And from today on you are uninvolved, is that understood? Whatever the mystery, I will unravel it. Despite your avowed cowardice, you seem to have a disastrous habit of leaping into dangerous situations without looking. I am beginning to have more sympathy for your poor cousin Henry than I would ever have expected."

14

Under the circumstances, Alessia thought it best not to apprise Rhys of her next movements. She waited a few days, then paid a second call on Mrs. Lewisham.

Luckily her daughter had returned, and the old nurse, freed from her responsibilities, greeted Alessia with obvious pleasure. She was quite willing to engage in further discussion about her favorite nursling, and under prompting was able to remember two more highly interesting pieces of information.

The first was that, now that she came to think of it, the quarrels between Lord Edward and his brother had seemed to increase after the visit of the strange man with the rocks. The second was that Mrs. Lewisham, fetching some medicine to Lord Edward in the midst of one of these quarrels, had caught a glimpse of paper that Lord Walter was waving about. She noticed it only because he had seemed irritated that she had seen it, and quickly put it away.

Alessia tried to control her growing excitement. "Can you remember anything about it—anything at all? A word that might have caught your eye, or who might have written it?"

But Mrs. Lewisham had had no more than a glimpse of it. She only knew it had left his late lordship almost apoplectic with rage, and that he had ordered his brother to throw the damned thing in the fire and not come brandishing it in his face again. He would never change his mind, not for a dozen fortunes.

"Those were his exact words?" Alessia pressed, her pulse beginning to race.

"Oh, yes. I may be getting on in years, but I've an excellent memory still. He said he'd never change his mind, not for a dozen fortunes. I thought it strange at the time, but then other things happened, and I must admit I hadn't thought of it since. Do you think it might be important?"

"I don't know. Did you ever see that letter again, or perhaps know where it might be found?"

"Why, I daresay it's still in the safe in the library, where his lordship put it."

Alessia was disappointed despite herself. "A safe?"

"Yes, but the key to it was always kept in the desk there in the library," offered Mrs. Lewisham calmly.

Alessia looked up quickly at the old woman, wondering how much she had guessed, and trying to keep her own triumph from showing. "Mrs. Lewisham, I could kiss you! In fact I think I will."

Mrs. Lewisham received the embrace with gratifying readiness, her old eyes beginning to twinkle. "I think I may live to dandle Master Rhys's children on my knees yet," she remarked obliquely, and left it at that.

Alessia went away, torn between excitement and the fear she had revealed too much to the old nurse. She consoled herself with the belief that Mrs. Lewisham seemed devoted to Rhys and would keep her mouth shut. But it worried her that now someone else knew of the possible plot and might, however inadvertently, give it away.

But to Alessia's credit, she did not even hesitate about what her next step must be. A month ago she would undoubtedly have been horrified at the very idea of breaking into someone else's safe to get her hands on a vital piece of evidence; but now she did not even blanch. And it would be far better to get it over at once, both to keep from having to think about it too much and to prevent Rhys getting wind of what she intended.

Admittedly her heart was beating a little fast when she once more presented herself at Crickfield. Luckily Lord Walter had indeed left instructions that she was to be given free rein of the library if she ever cared to return, for she was admitted without question. And even more fortunate, she was informed that Lord Walter was himself away from home and would be sorry to have missed her.

Alessia doubted that, but wasted no time in repairing to the library, declining all offers of refreshment. She made up some excuse of having overlooked some obscure reference she had meant to copy the last time she was there, but she could tell the young footman who admitted her was wholly incurious.

She thought he would no doubt have been profoundly shocked to learn her real purpose, and hoped no one ever would.

In order to maintain her pose of somewhat foolish spinster, she was careful to spread out two or three volumes on the table and make a few notes. One, a copy of Gray's translation of the first canto of the *Divine Comedy,* proved highly interesting, and she found herself wishing she could have shown it to her father. The other two were merely for show, but she worked diligently for some time, spreading papers about her and making it look as if she were lost in her research.

She made herself waste nearly an hour in this fashion, waiting to see if her host might materialize, feeling himself duty-bound to come and speak to her. But no one disturbed her, and she could only hope that she had been forgotten by the busy staff.

At last she rose, her heart beginning to quicken despite her conviction that she ran very little danger of being discovered, and went about her real business there.

She found the safe easily enough, behind a walnut panel, for Mrs. Lewisham had told her where to look for it. And sure enough, when she looked, the key was in a drawer of the desk as the nurse had described it.

It seemed a casual arrangement for so valuable a document, and that shook her for a moment. But then she told herself his lordship must feel himself safe enough. The servants would hardly pry, and no one else was looking for it.

Her hands shook a little as she lifted the key into the lock of the safe, but she was unaware she was holding her breath until the key turned easily and the safe swung open on well-oiled hinges.

Then she let it out in a rush, wondering, now that the moment had come, if she looked as absurdly guilty as she felt.

But it was far too late for such scruples, and so she made herself go methodically through the papers in the safe. It seemed to her exaggerated sensibilities that her heart was beating so loudly that everyone in the house must be able to hear it. But nobody came, and the library remained quiet and peaceful.

There was a number of documents, and she glanced hurriedly through most of them, trying to keep her haste from making her clumsy. Most seemed to have to do with nothing more suspicious than rents and household expenditures, and at first she thought the mysterious letter wasn't here after all.

Her heart plummeted, and she had almost given up when she discovered, at the bottom of the pile, a thin sheet of paper that seemed to be a letter addressed to Lord Walter.

She scanned it rapidly, her heart rising as quickly as it had fallen. It seemed to be from one Grenville Maltby, who wrote civilly to thank Lord Walter for his kind hospitality, and confirmed the analyses of the ore samples he had taken away with him. It seemed that all samples had shown a high content of copper, as he had suspected, and from the readiness with which they had been found on the surface of the estate, Mr. Maltby felt sure a rich vein lay underneath the property. As they had discussed, the war and subsequent increased demand for metals had very much improved the profitability of mining copper, and if his lordship and his brother cared to pursue such a commercial undertaking, Mr. Maltby was sure he would find it profitable. He remained, his, etc., Grenville Maltby.

Alessia was so caught up in the triumph of finally discovering the motive she had been searching for that she didn't hear the door open, or sense the presence of anyone else in the room until it was almost too late.

Then she heard a quick step, and thrust the letter back into the safe, her hands shaking in earnest now and her heart racing.

Luckily the safe was located behind one of the bays, and she had already made sure she was not visible from the door. She closed the betraying safe door with her body, and could only pray that it would stay closed and was not one of those that had to be locked again with a key. Then she plunged the key into the pocket of her skirt, at the same time reaching for a book on the shelf nearest her and pretending to be engrossed in it.

Then, as the footsteps came nearer, and seemed to falter, as if the newcomer was wondering where she could have gotten to, she peered round the bay and said foolishly, "Is someone there? I thought I heard . . . Oh!"

She did indeed jump then, for she recognized the man immediately as Rhys's cousin Owen. He was a good-looking young man of some thirty years, with a pleasant, open expression. She emerged, feeling even more foolish, and said, "I beg your pardon, but you startled me! Dear me, how awkward this is. Lord Walter gave me permission to pore through his really most remarkable library, and I'm afraid I've quite lost track of the time. I am Miss Fielding, you know. My father was Sir William Fielding, the noted scholar. I was just admiring this remarkable book on the early Italian Renaissance."

She could only pray that Owen Fitzwarren was no better a scholar than his father, for the book she had grabbed had nothing at all to do with the Italian Renaissance.

Luckily he scarcely glanced at it. "Er . . . how nice. I'm afraid I've never bothered to properly appreciate the library here," he said, somewhat at a loss. "And I know who you are, Miss Fielding, for Father told me you might come again. I am Owen Fitzwarren, you know."

She shook hands with him, still a little shaken and longing to escape. Rhys liked and admired his cousin, and she could see why, for he looked very different from his father. He had an easy manner and none of the coldness that made Lord Walter Fitzwarren so unpleasant. But at that moment she had no desire to make his acquaintance, especially with the key to the safe burning guiltily in her pocket and the feeling that the knowledge she had discovered must be blazoned on her forehead for all to see.

Even so, she found herself liking Owen Fitzwarren. He inquired civilly after her research, confessed to being no scholar himself, and seemed disposed to want to talk.

She had drifted away from the safe, fearing something there might betray her. But after a while, when he continued to make polite conversation and did not loudly accuse her of breaking into his father's safe, she began to relax a little.

She had quite forgotten her self-assigned role, however, and afterward could only hope Mr. Owen Fitzwarren never compared notes about her with his father.

He told her he had arrived only the day before, and on questioning, admitted to having little taste for Crickfield. He much preferred his own home near Oxford, but then, tastes were different. He had never cared much for all that decayed splendor.

"Yes, but it is really quite splendid, you know," Alessia said truthfully. "Your father was kind enough to allow me a tour earlier, and I very much enjoyed it."

"Oh, yes, it's well enough, I'll grant you. My cousin and I used to call it the Mausoleum." Abruptly a shadow seemed to cross his face, and then he made an effort to shake it off. "But I shouldn't complain, I suppose. One shouldn't look a gift horse in the mouth and all that."

He looked so rueful when he said it, however, that her last reservations melted. "Yes, I understand your uncle left the estate to your father over the claims of his own son. I must confess it seems rather unusual."

His pleasant mouth twisted. "Not if you'd known my uncle. I've seldom known a more headstrong, stubborn man. Unless it would be my cousin Rhys, of course. Oh, well, it's done now. I doubt if Rhys will ever return. He hated the place even more than I did."

"And if he should?" she asked curiously.

"I would be delighted, of course. I . . . My father inherited the estate, not me, you know. But once it's mine, I . . . well . . . " Then he shrugged, apparently aware he was saying too much to a stranger. "I suppose it's useless to say what I will do so far in the future. But for my part, I wish my uncle Edward had never left the wretched place to us. And I am undoubtedly boring you. I only came, you know, to see if you would take some refreshment. The footman tells me you've been closeted in here for hours, slaving over your books."

She felt even more embarrassed, but declined any refreshment. "The truth is, I'm about finished now. I have only one or two more notes to make, and then I'll be going. In fact I should have been gone long since, for it's later than I thought. If I'm not careful, it will be dark before I get home, and that will be annoying, for my cousin is expecting me."

He took the hint and did not remain much longer, merely politely repeating his father's hope that she would come and use the library often. "The next time, I hope I may persuade you to abandon your studies, for at least a brief while, and take pity on me. I don't know many people in the district, you know, and would count it a kindness in you to spend an hour or so with me."

By that time she was indeed aware of the lateness of the hour, and wanted only to be gone, but that opened up new questions in her mind, and she made herself say curiously, "Oh, are you meaning to remain, then?"

Again a shadow seemed to cross his eyes, but he gave her one of his grave, pleasant smiles. "I confess, until today that prospect had filled me with little happiness, but now I am more resigned to it. But my father seems to feel it his duty to remain, at least for the moment, and I don't like to leave him. I'm sure you know how that is, Miss Fielding."

She agreed to it, and as if sensing her growing impatience, he took himself off. As soon as he was out the door, she rushed anxiously to make sure of the safe, restore the key to its drawer, and reassure herself that everything was exactly at it had been before.

She then made herself go back to her books for another quarter of an hour, since she had said she had a few more notes to make. It required almost all of her willpower, for her nerves were screaming by then, and for once she found it impossible to force her mind to a scholarly attention.

For despite everything she could do, it insisted upon returning again and again to the letter now safely back where it belonged, and its deadly portent.

15

Alessia left Crickfield for the second time in a far more turbulent state of mind than she had the first time.

She had proved beyond a possible doubt that Lord Walter Fitzwarren had a considerable motive for wanting his nephew's inheritance. She had been searching for a motive, and might even have suspected what she would find, but the proof still shook her. No longer did it all seem a somewhat agreeably exciting game to her. Now that she realized exactly how deadly serious it was, and how much danger Rhys still stood in, her heart seemed to have lodged permanently somewhere in her throat, and she could not wait to get home again and assure herself of his safety.

Reaction was definitely setting in as well. Before, she had anticipated only a certain degree of embarrassment had she been discovered. Now that she knew how much Lord Walter had to hide, embarrassment seemed the least of her worries. Nor did the knowledge do anything to steady her.

She had driven herself in her father's phaeton that morning, Jane having needed the services of Horsham. Now she regretted the absence of his solid presence. Her own hands were none too reliable on the reins at the moment.

No doubt now remained in her mind that Lord Walter, having discovered the hidden wealth of Crickfield, had somehow managed to have his nephew disinherited. Whether the will had been obtained under undue persuasion or was an outright forgery, she didn't know, of course. But at this point she would put nothing past his cold lordship.

Obviously he had not expected his nephew to return and threaten all his carefully laid plans. With a disinherited Rhys back in England and asking awkward questions, however, it must have seemed that the sudden discovery of valuable copper on the property would look too suspicious.

He had thus been faced with the difficult choice of either having to delay the development of so valuable an asset or removing his troublesome nephew. And it was not hard to see which Lord Walter had chosen.

Nor must there have seemed to be very much risk to him. According to Rhys, only the solicitor and one or two casual acquaintances had known he was back in England. Had his body turned up, the victim of a robbery, it was doubtful he would ever have been identified. Even if he had been, no one would have bothered to ask too many questions after all those years.

With the possible exception of Owen Fitzwarren. She had liked him, and found it impossible to believe he knew what his father was planning. But then, it little mattered, for the property had been left to his father, not to him.

It was all exceedingly neat, except that Lord Walter had underestimated his nephew's will to survive. It was also appallingly cold-blooded. Abruptly she shivered and urged her team on, for once in the last six months in a hurry to be home again.

When she reached Horsham's cottage, however, she discovered that contrary to orders, Rhys had gone for a stroll in the grounds, and she had to track him down.

The weather had warmed, and she could not blame him for his dissatisfaction with his continued inactivity. But in her present mood, any delay in finding him and making sure he was safe tore at her nerves. He had also, she saw when she finally spotted him, removed his arm from its sling and thrust it through the belt of his rustic jacket.

He saw her driving toward him, and came swinging across the fields to meet her, looking disgustingly healthy. He grinned as he reached her, and complained, "It seems I've been inactive for months, not a few weeks, for I am shockingly out of shape."

"In reaction to which you tramp for miles in a sharp north wind, risking undoing all your progress!" she retorted, unable to prevent a little of her anxiety showing through.

He stood looking up at her, beginning to frown a little. But he said merely, "I have been idle more than long enough. But never mind that. Were you looking for me or merely out for an afternoon's drive?"

"Looking for you. Get in. If we are seen, I have only to say I saw you out walking and took pity on you, and this will be a private place for us to talk."

He glanced at her again quickly, but obligingly climbed in, looking only a little awkward because of his weak right arm, and settled beside her. "I confess I much prefer riding to walking, any day. Which reminds me, I met your cousin Jane earlier. I very kindly opened the gate for her carriage, but was rewarded with a scowl and her best lady-of-the-manor air. I must admit I didn't take to her."

Alessia was too preoccupied to pay much attention. "At least it's gratifying to know she did go out in the carriage. I suspected her of having invented an excuse just because I asked if I could borrow it."

He grinned at her. "Well, she had a pair of extremely bracket-faced children with her, so I assume she was going out visiting. But I wouldn't be surprised if she formed the plan after you asked her for the use of the carriage, not before. She's obviously jealous of you."

Her problems with Jane seemed very unimportant at the moment. "She has no need, and that was petty of me. It is her carriage, after all, and she has no need to make up an excuse for using it. But that isn't what I want to talk to you about, and you know it."

"Yes, ma'am," he answered meekly. "You've a pretty hand with the ribbons, by the way. Usually I don't care for women drivers, but I watched you come up the drive, and Horsham's right. You've a light hand and a sure touch. Cousin Jane can't have seen you drive, or she'd far prefer to lend you her carriage rather than have you take the shine out of her by driving yourself."

She failed even to smile at this sally, all her earlier fears rushing to overcome her. It had belatedly occurred to her that she had absolutely no idea how he would take the news. He had so far humored her in her suspicions and seemed to be merely amused, not offended at her accusations against his relations. But he had himself remained skeptical, and she was unable to tell how fond he actually might be of his uncle, or how he would greet proof that a member of his own family had plotted to have him killed.

As if sensing some of her agitation, he reached over and took the reins from her. "Let me have that. You seem oddly preoccupied, and I am quite capable of driving such a docile pair one-handed. Now, what is it? You obviously have something on your mind, so out with it. Has Cousin Jane been plaguing you again? Don't try to bamboozle me that something isn't wrong, for I can tell there is."

She looked at him then, and was struck with how much a part of her life he had become in so short a time. He was more familiar to her and far more comfortable than any of her family, certainly; and even of the few friends she possessed. She had a sudden vision of what her life would be like without him, and it shook her badly.

His expression had grown a little quizzical at her delay in answering; but something of her fear must have shown in her eyes, for he smiled then, in a way that made her heart accelerate for a very different reason. "What is it, Angel?" he asked quietly, no longer teasing her. "You can tell me."

She thought then that the oddest thing was that she could. At the moment she could think of nothing that she wouldn't be able to tell him, however shocking or shameful.

Unless it was that his uncle had once tried to kill him for his inheritance, and almost certainly would do so again.

Her courage nearly deserted her then. "Oh, dear, this is harder than I had anticipated," she said weakly.

She thought he stiffened, and there was a certain fine tension about his eyes, but he merely said in amusement, "Yes, you were ever the coward, as you say. Let me help you, then. You are trying to tell me, as delicately and politely as possible, that I have outstayed my welcome."

It was so far from what she had been thinking that she responded instinctively, and perhaps far too vehemently. "*Good God, no!* In fact, if you must know, I was just thinking that I don't know how I managed to get along without you to unburden myself on and vent my frustrations."

She thought he relaxed slightly, but he shrugged, his eyes on the road ahead. "You underestimate yourself shockingly, as I've told you before. But if not that, what is it?"

Seeing no other way, she took a deep breath and blurted it out—her visit to Mrs. Lewisham and the information of the letter she had let drop, the subsequent return to Crickfield and her deliberate breaking into the safe, even the meeting with his cousin.

He heard her out in unrevealing silence, and she once again had reason to curse his ability to hide his thoughts. She could not tell, as she spoke, whether he was shocked, surprised, or angry.

Only in the end did he surprise her by putting his head back and beginning to laugh. When she looked offended, he managed to say, "Sorry! I'm not laughing at you, Angel! In fact I'm grateful to you, even though I distinctly recall forbidding you to do anything more. But we'll discuss that later! For the moment I can't help remembering what a consummate coward you are! Far too timid to stand up to your own relations in fact."

She grinned a little at that. "Well, that is a very different thing, and you know it. And I had no notion then that I might really be in danger, of course, or I daresay I might have thought better of it. But don't change the subject. I have proved that your uncle had every reason to wish you out of the way—and still does. Even I know that since the war the price of most metals has gone sky-high. If there is indeed a rich vein of copper on Crickfield, you have been cheated out of a fortune."

"Yes, so it would seem. And that is almost the funniest part of all."

When she looked a question, he want on, "Even if my father had known that he was sitting on a gold mine . . . er . . . a copper mine, rather, and he could have the means to sink all the money he wanted into the damned place, he wouldn't have done it. That was doubtless what he and my uncle argued over so violently at the end. You see, no Fitzwarren would ever engage in such a vulgarly commercial enterprise as mining."

She found it far from amusing. "Then that may explain why he tried to send for you at the last. It . . . it also means," she added faintly, a chill running up her spine, "that your uncle may have . . . prevented him from doing so or having an opportunity to make a new will. In which case his death may not have been in the least natural."

He did sober slightly at that. "Yes, I must admit the fact is becoming a distinct possibility."

She shivered in the cold wind. "It's horrible. But whether or not you can prove there is copper beneath Crickfield, the fact remains that your father didn't make a new will, and that it all belongs legally to your uncle. He would seem to have won. Worse, even I will concede that it all sounds so farfetched that few will ever believe you."

"That does present a problem, doesn't it?" he agreed in amusement.

"Don't! Don't joke about it. Even if he did murder your father and try to murder you, how will you ever be able to prove it? And once it's known you're alive, your uncle can try again to remove you whenever he chooses. I almost wish now I had never meddled!"

"So do I—but for a very different reason. But never mind that. And at any rate, you must admit it would simplify things," he retorted cheerfully. "If my uncle succeeded in murdering me, you could probably make the charges stick."

She shivered. "It's not funny. What . . . what do you mean to do?"

"Ah, an interesting question, that. And one I don't have an answer to, just yet. But I do know one thing I'm going to do, and that immediately: remove myself to an inn and retire you as fellow conspirator. I never did like it, and now that I know the truth, however grateful I may be to you for discovering it, you will have nothing more to do with any of this. And believe me, I'm not making idle threats this time. I will go straight to Cousin Henry if I have to to enforce it."

"You needn't worry. I am repaid, for if I hadn't meddled, none of this might ever have been discovered," she said bitterly. "You would have gone back to Europe in safety and been perfectly satisfied."

"Yes, but a good deal poorer, you must admit!"

"Does the possibility of a great deal of money mean that much to you?"

He laughed. "It's bound to change things somewhat, sweetheart. A drafty mausoleum that's nothing but a yoke round my neck is very different from a fortune underground."

"Yes, but I've been thinking," she said unhappily. "Even if you should prove your uncle tried to murder you, unless you can prove as well that your father's will was illegal, your cousin will still inherit Crickfield, not you. It all seems hopeless, I must confess."

"And regrettably, I haven't exactly helped my case by disappearing for the last six years," he admitted ruefully.

"Then you don't mean to fight it?" she asked almost hopefully. She had been the one to insist from the beginning that his uncle must be behind the attempt on his life. But she had had ample time in the drive home to realize how dangerous her careless meddling might be. And the truth was, she would far prefer him to return abroad and leave his uncle in possession than see him in further danger, which he would be if he started questioning events.

"I don't know. My father called me a care-for-naught, and I suppose it's true. I spent six years with scarcely a thought for what I'd left behind, and my inheritance seemed far more of a millstone than a windfall. I had long ago decided I wanted nothing to do with permanence and respectability. Those six years I spent drifting were the most pleasant I can remember. I touched few people and no one touched me. I even lent my name for a day—a few months even—to various causes, but none of it ever really mattered. The truth is, I have never accepted any responsibility, and I don't know if I'm capable of it. Or if I care enough to try," he said honestly. "But I'll admit that it sticks in my craw to let him get by with it."

Then he smiled down into her trouble eyes. "And I fear you set me a hard example to follow, you know."

"*I* do?" she asked in bewilderment.

"Yes, you. You don't hesitate to throw your heart to lost souls and lost causes. And I suspect you wouldn't hesitate a moment if faced with the same choice."

She blushed as her eyes fell away. "You flatter me. I told you I only stayed to help you because I was longing for an excuse not to return home. And this—I had no idea what I was risking. I suspect it was no more than a foolish game to me. Now that I know differently . . ." She shuddered again and wrapped her cloak more tightly about her.

"Yes, ever the consummate coward," he said lightly.

They were silent then, each busy with his own thoughts. Only as they drew up to the dower house did she dare to ask, dreading the answer she would receive, whatever it was, "What do you intend to do?"

He grinned ruefully. "Why, go to London and interview one Grenville Maltby, of course. I may indeed decide to do nothing, but at least I intend to have all the facts first."

16

Rhys took the mail coach to London, relieved to be active once more, even if on such a wild-goose chase. There he wasted no time in retrieving his trunks, more grateful than he would once have believed possible to be restored to the estate of a gentleman.

Then he sought out one Grenville Maltby.

He succeeded in finding him without much difficulty, but had more trouble convincing the stolid Mr. Maltby to part with the information he sought.

Mr. Maltby's hesitation seemed to stem more from ethical considerations than from any reluctance to reveal the results of his study, for he seemed the sort of upright, unimaginative man it was almost impossible to believe could be in on such a scheme.

But Rhys had taken the precaution of reuniting himself not only with his wardrobe but also with the bulk of his cash, and that, along with his obvious knowledge of Mr. Maltby's report, at last convinced the mining engineer to loosen his tongue.

He remembered the job very well, of course. Yes, in his opinion there could be little doubt that a substantial copper vein lay under the hills of Crickfield. It was often that way, for ore was usually to be found in land that was suitable for no other purpose and most had long despaired of.

When asked if it wasn't unusual to find copper in an area not noted for mining of any sort, he readily agreed to it. But then, Mr. Fitzwarren might remember the Anglesey mines discovered at the turn of the century, which had revolutionized the copper industry. Ah, he knew very little about copper? Mr. Maltby wasn't surprised, for very few people did. But really, it was a most interesting specialty. And copper could be found almost anywhere, you know, not just in Cornwall.

When asked if he thought it worth developing, Mr. Maltby pursed his lips and refused to be pinned down. He had informed Lord Walter Fitzwarren that he believed so, but of course it was impossible to tell without more exploration. As to a possible value on the copper, that he would not even venture to guess. He thought it might be substantial, but of course it would take considerable capital to develop, and it was never possible to predict how rich a vein might be. That was what made copper mining so fascinating. If one could simply pick it up from the ground, obviously it would not be nearly so valuable.

He ventured a smile at this last mild jest, but would commit himself no further. As to the destruction of the land necessary to mine copper, of course it was an industry, as any other. Had Mr. Fitzwarren ever traveled in Cornwall? Then he would know something of what was entailed. Fortunately, newer engines and methods had made it a far more profitable enterprise than it was used to be, and of course the war had raised prices considerably. But it was certainly not an attractive undertaking, any more than an iron manufactory in one's garden would be, and there was little use in pretending otherwise.

Had Mr. Maltby himself ever spoken directly to Lord Edward Fitzwarren about the possibility of copper being found at Crickfield? At that his usually stolid expression altered to one of remembered annoyance. Yes, indeed he had. In his defense, Lord Edward had, Mr. Fitzwarren must understand, obviously not been well, and indeed Mr. Maltby believed he had died not long afterward. But he had also been most violently opposed to any exploration of copper on his estate, and said so in terms that were as uncompromising as they were rude. One met that now and then, of course, especially in the older generation. It did little good to point out to such men that if the vein proved rich enough they might build themselves as many houses as they might wish in place of the ones they were despoiling. But then, Mr. Maltby had discovered that "progress" was not a word that some men ever adjusted to.

Rhys thanked him and went thoughtfully away, not certain he was any better off than when he had come. Possible copper of an indeterminate value requiring considerable outlay to discover seemed vague enough, but as a motive for murder, almost hopeless. He could believe his father had set his mind against it from the outset, but was his uncle certain enough—or desperate enough—to risk so much on so ephemeral a reward?

He received one part of his answer much sooner than he had expected. As he was strolling back from a leisurely dinner that evening he unexpectedly ran into his cousin Newby in the middle of Piccadilly.

Lord Newby, eldest son of the Earl of Petworth, had always been a large, vague young man of little brains but kindly intent. His father, the cause, by the mere fact of his existence, of so much of Rhys's and his cousin Owen's unhappiness as children, had barely common sense, and of the three brothers was by far the least impressive. His children tended all to be equally slow-witted, but Rhys had always had a soft spot for his cousin Newby.

When he had left six years ago, Newby had been on the point of marriage to a colorless young woman of excellent family who was even more boring than he was. By virtue of his future title, Newby had been a prize target on the matrimonial mart, and had been plagued by the machinations of highly ambitious mamas more concerned with obtaining titles for their daughters than husbands with common sense. In the end he had willingly acceded to his father's handpicked candidate, if only to get some peace, for he was terrified of the relentless lures cast out to him.

At the time, Rhys had felt vaguely sorry for him, and been glad he himself had so little to interest matchmaking mamas. Now he discovered that although Newby looked a good deal more than six years older, and considerably heavier, in the interim he seemed to have acquired a certain and rather unexpected dignity.

He looked childishly delighted to meet his cousin, however, and insisted upon taking him off to his house for a drink. "No idea you were home, dear boy!" he said genially. "No idea at all. In fact, given the state of things, suspected . . . Well, never mind that. Sorry about your father, of course. Always fond of him, you know. But enough of that. What the devil happened to your arm?"

"Oh, a slight accident. It's all but healed now. How have you been?"

It soon developed that Newby, besides developing a paunch, had produced three offspring as well, two girls and a boy. "The boy's a spit of myself at that age, I'm afraid, poor little devil," he admitted gloomily. "But luckily the girls take after their mother. You've never married? No, I suppose you wouldn't have. I must admit you never seemed inclined in that direction. Never thought I was myself, if it comes to that, but can't say that I regret it. Solidity and all that."

Rhys thought that marriage suited his cousin, and grinningly told him so. Newby took it as a simple compliment. "Aye, but Mary—you remember Mary, of course?—has taken the children into the country. As a matter of fact, I'm delighted I met you, for the house always seems a bit empty when they're away, don't you know? Full of servants, of course, but it's not the same thing."

Newby rattled on in his vague way about old acquaintances and the family, and it was only after several glasses of brandy that Rhys finally managed to draw him onto the subject of his father's will.

Newby looked uncomfortable. "Aye, devilish thing to have happened," he said frankly. "But not so surprising, really. Should have come home sooner, dear boy," he added simply. "Always said so."

"So I'm beginning to agree," Rhys admitted wryly. "You believe the will was genuine, then?"

Newby looked surprised. "Genuine? Is there any doubt? I mean . . . passed through any number of attorneys' hands, I suppose. They're bound to have found it out if it weren't genuine. At any rate, I saw Uncle Edward myself only a few months before he died. Same as always, only in even worse temper if you ask me, but while I don't wish to wound you, old boy, he was still pretty full of what he referred to as your betrayal. Called you a damned wastrel and swore never to have you on the place again. Never really thought he'd cut you out completely, of course, for I always privately thought his bark was worse than his bite. But then, if it comes to that, you never wanted to be lumbered with the place anyway, did you? I certainly never thought so."

Rhys grinned at him and accepted a pinch of

snuff. "I never thought so either. Tell me, Francis, do you really want to be lumbered with Petworth?" he asked curiously. "I've often wondered."

Newby looked even more surprised at the question. "Never really thought about it, I guess. Can't get out of it, so no good in thinking about it, is there? At any rate, it's something I've lived with all my life."

"And there speaks the true Englishman. I suppose it's never ever occurred to you that such houses have long since outlasted their usefulness? Most have caused far more heartaches than good, and along with inherited titles and the idea that one man is better than another because of his birth, have much to answer for."

"I can see you haven't changed," said Newby comfortably. "Always were a fireband. I can't help thinking where the world would be if everyone felt as you did, though."

Rhys laughed. "You're probably right. Never mind. I haven't yet seen any of the rest of the family. Do you see Owen much? Or Uncle Walter?"

"I see Owen every now and then, of course. Like you, he claims to want nothing to do with Crickfield. Insists he don't begin to understand what bee his father has in his bonnet over it, for it's never been profitable, of course. As for Uncle Walter, he's the same as always, I daresay. Though I did hear, in an out-of-the-way fashion, that he was a trifle run off his legs. No idea how much truth there may be in it, of course."

When pressed, he could tell Rhys little more than that. One does hear things, of course, without remembering quite where. It seemed to him it was something about bad investments, but then, he might be mistaken. In fact it would be just like him to have the whole thing twisted round, and it had been about someone else entirely. Rhys knew that he'd never had any head for business.

Rhys had to be content with that. They spent another comfortable hour reminiscing about their childhood and mutual acquaintances, and when Rhys finally strolled home in the early hours of the morning, it was to the reflection that he had enjoyed seeing his cousin again more than he would ever have expected.

He also felt oddly regretful, though over what, he couldn't quite pin down.

In the meantime, with Rhys gone, Alessia's life gradually resumed its former pattern. She thought it was an unwelcome foretaste of what it would be like when he finally left for good.

Reassured by what she saw as Alessia's return to normalcy, Clarissa went happily about, chattering and driving Alessia more and more frequently into hiding in her study. But there she found she paid very little attention to Dante and her father's work. Instead she spent far too much time thinking of an untidy golden head and an irreverent face, and tried not to imagine it lying dead somewhere on the road to London.

The weather had warmed to an unseasonable March, and Jane, having decided to undertake what she called an overdue spring cleaning, ruthlessly enlisted Clarissa and Alessia to help turn out all the rooms.

Alessia was glad enough to keep busy, and watched without a pang as all the old, intimately familiar rooms were rearranged and the last of her presence at the Oaks obliterated. She was surprised at her lack of reaction, but it was as if she had belatedly had to acknowledge that it was no longer her home and would never be again.

After considering it, she realized she had Rhys to thank for that. Once he was back and his affairs had been settled, she thought she would finally find the courage to leave and start a new life for herself.

The only problem was, of course, she was no longer certain exactly what she would be fleeing from: her old memories or far more recent ones.

Rhys had been gone a little over a week, and she had no word from him, when she finally received a hand-delivered note. It read:

> Got back this morning. Discovered some very interesting facts in London. Meet me in the old carriage house at four.
>
> R.

She had not yet seen his handwriting, but it was as bold as she might have expected. The old carriage house was near Horsham's cottage, but isolated enough to ensure privacy, and now housed little but castoffs. As a meeting place it was excellent, but she wondered what he could have discovered to necessitate so much secrecy.

At a little before the appointed hour she let herself out of the house and walked briefly to the rendezvous, her heart beating a little fast despite all she could do. She had missed him more than she would have thought possible, for just the knowledge of his presence somehow seemed to help. She had discovered that almost anything could be borne, from Clarissa's incessant chatter to Jane's petty revenges, so long as she could repeat it to him and expect his teasing response, putting it all into perspective.

It was not yet dusk, but the sun was beginning to set and the cold wind to pick up, and for a moment she regretted not having brought a heavier cloak. The carriage house, when she reached it, looked gloomy in the late-afternoon light. The heavy doors were closed, so that it was impossible to tell if he had gotten there before her. She shivered a little, cravenly hoping he had and that she wouldn't be obliged to wait for him in so depressing a place.

She knew from experience that inside it was musty-smelling and full of cobwebs and dust, for it had been used for little more than storage for years. Even in high summer, the last time she had been inside, it had been dark and gloomy. She didn't like to think what it would be like on an early-spring afternoon. In fact she began to wish she had thought to bring a lantern with her.

Then she saw with relief that the bolt was unfastened and realized that Rhys must indeed be there before her. Without any more hesitation she pushed open the heavy door and hurried in.

It took a moment for her eyes to adjust to the darker interior, and when they did, she could not immediately see him. She advanced a few paces, feeling her way, and called out to him.

There was no answer. She hesitated, despite herself beginning to feel a frisson down her spine, and half-turned back toward the open door and its inviting square of light. It was foolish to be afraid, but she had never liked the place and she had an odd feeling of unease now.

Again she told herself she was overreacting, but still thought she would wait outside. There were bound to be rats there, if nothing else, and she had no desire to encounter one in the dark.

She had started toward the door when a slight sound reached her. Before she could react, something came crashing down on the back of her head and she knew no more.

17

Rhys returned to the Oaks, reflecting as he rode through the countryside on how quickly he had begun to feel at home in England again. At first it had seemed strange to be back especially since he had left in the first place because he found English life hopelessly confining.

Perhaps he would again, but for the moment he had to admit it was both familiar and refreshingly new, and had a charm all its own he had not found in all his wanderings. Worse, he had even found himself feeling jealous of his stolid cousin's life.

But that way lay danger. The attempt on his life, the surprising possibility of a fortune beneath Crickfield, the almost insurmountable problem of proving his uncle a murderer and disproving his own father's will—unfortunately none of that added up to any promise of certainty or stability. Nothing really had changed.

Before, he had never wanted any certainty or stability in his life, preferring never to know what tomorrow would bring. Certainly he had never wanted Crickfield. It was because of Crickfield that he and his father had quarreled so often. Because of Crickfield he had been kept on a continually short rein, with never as much money as the other boys, or, after he had left school, the income to become a young man-about-town, as his friends were doing.

For the first time it occurred to him in amusement that Crickfield had been a rival all his life, a sort of older brother who took all his father's love and attention. It had certainly demanded so much that there had never been enough left over of either for anyone else.

The thought saddened him as well. Even in the end his father had chosen Crickfield over his only son. It was typical that he also chose it over a potential fortune. It had in fact become his mausoleum—a monument to useless and overweening pride.

And if it were his? Did he hate it so much that he would gladly see it demolished under the ugly demands of copper mining?

But that was a fool's pastime, for it was unlikely ever to be his. As foolish as wishing for the moon and stars—or an angel, he thought wryly, and tried to put an end to such useless speculations.

He still had no idea what he intended to do. The ugly scandal if he accused his uncle, the long, drawn-out legal battles, the endless waiting for others to ponderously decide his future—he wasn't sure he had the stomach for it. Nor was he at all sure of eventual success, for his uncle was clever and the evidence against him circumstantial at best. And in the meantime he would be stuck in England, cooling his heels, with no certainty of success and no right to plan for the future.

That word again. The only certainty he had ever wanted was the certainty he didn't know where he was going to be six months from now; and the only plans he had ever made involved which inaccessible place he was going to go next. It was ridiculous to let a highly speculative fortune and a black-eyed angel change that.

He resisted the recurring fantasy of introducing Alessia to the place of her birth, with its warm sun and warmer wine and its passion. To showing her all the places he loved most in the world, knowing she would make a boon traveling companion. He had resisted companions before—and certainly women—but he did not have to be told that she would never tire or complain. However many days—and nights—he spent in her company would never be enough.

But that way lay madness. As mad as to regret a heritage so carelessly thrown away, or the years spent running away from himself.

He was glad to reach his destination, if for no other reason than to put an end to such useless thoughts. But he was surprised at how much at home he felt by now in the country of his birth.

A highly relieved Mrs. Horsham greeted him. "Oh, there you are," she cried. "Did you have a successful journey? I was expecting you, as it happens, for Miss Alessia sent word earlier and asked if you would be so good as to meet her in the old coach house at four. It's nearly that now, so you'll have to hurry."

He was surprised, for he had not let her know he was coming. Then he reflected ruefully how well the country grapevine worked, and dismissed it. "Yes, thank you, Mrs. Horsham." He meant to remove himself to an inn, but he had wanted to see Alessia first and tell her of his discovery. What he meant to do after that, he still had no idea.

He had not yet changed back into his new identity, and had for the moment forgotten that Mrs. Horsham had never seen him in his true guise. Now he saw her looking at him as if she scarcely recognized him, and it seemed to fluster her a little. "Oh, dear, sir. Here you are looking so much the gentleman I'm a little embarrassed, to tell the truth," she confessed. "You've always been so free and easy in your manners that I somehow forgot that you wasn't one of us. I only hope I haven't offended you in some way."

He was sorry, and hoped he managed to smooth things over. She had from the first insisted upon calling him sir, and treating him as an honored guest in her home, but over the days his common clothes and easy manners had gradually relaxed her awkwardness, and she had begun in truth to treat him almost like the nephew he pretended to be.

Now he could see with regret that she had been reminded of his birth, and stiffened up again. He sighed, and as he had so often done in his travels, thought how ridiculous it was that worth should be measured by such superficial outward signs as birth and wealth.

He stayed chatting with her a little longer, wanting to ease her embarrassment, and was only reminded of the time by the chiming of the big hall clock striking the quarter-hour. "I'd better return to my other identity before anyone else sees me, if my old room is still available," he said, beginning to climb the stairs. "Have you any idea what Miss Fielding wanted to see me about?"

"No, though her ladyship's kept her hopping while you were gone, that I will say," said the good lady darkly. "I never thought to say so, but I would be glad to see her leave now, so I would. It's not right she should be displaced, and at the beck and call of one who's not fit to lick her bootlaces, and so I will maintain, no matter what Horsham says."

He had the feeling she was eyeing him almost expectantly, and for the second time found himself thrown out of countenance. Neither of the Horshams had ever questioned his presence there, but given what they knew, it would only be natural if they had their own thoughts on the subject.

Certainly they were more than fond of Alessia and had only her good at heart.

Unfortunately he could offer Mrs. Horsham no reassurance, and so merely said, too heartily, "Well, I must go. I will undoubtedly be back in time for supper, and hope I'm invited, for none of the London cooks can measure up to you."

She blushed and was successfully distracted, and he soon managed to escape to change swiftly and go in search of Alessia. But it was yet another indication that it was past time he was thinking of moving on.

The coach house, when he reached it, looked shut and uninhabited, but no premonition of disaster occurred to him. He pushed open the door with none of Alessia's hesitation, merely halting until his eyes adjusted to the interior gloom before advancing confidently in.

For a moment he saw nothing out of the ordinary. Only as the door abruptly swung shut behind him and he heard the bolt go home did he begin to suspect a trap. The sound seemed to echo through the empty building as if to reinforce the idea, and the interior to become much darker as the square of light from the door was cut off.

He hurried over and pounded uselessly, knowing even as he did so that no one would hear him. Even so, he was still not overly worried, for Mrs. Horsham knew where he was, and being locked in a little-used building seemed harmless enough.

It was then, as his eyes adjusted even more to the dim light, that he saw the ominous shape stretched out on the stone floor. In an instant he was bending over it, recognizing with a sort of sick inevitability the black dress and light cloak.

He feared at first she was dead, for she was cold

and very still. Then to his almost dizzy relief he at last managed to locate a pulse in her neck. He could see no sign of what had happened, or why she should be lying on the cold stone floor of a dark and empty building. But she was deeply unconscious and gave no flicker of awareness.

Even so he was still puzzled, for he could not see why they had both been lured there. It made no sense, for sooner or later they would be missed and a search begun for them.

Then all too soon the reason became painfully obvious. Even as he knelt on the stone floor trying to rouse Alessia, his ears became aware of a strange snapping sound.

At first he ignored it, but the darkness seemed inexplicably to lessen, and it wasn't long before the first flames began to shoot up. He saw then with horror that one entire side of the vacant building had been stacked with hay and odds and ends of highly flammable castoffs. Even as he watched, the flames began to spread hungrily.

He leapt up and tried frantically to smother them, using whatever he could find to hand and with little concern for his own vulnerable flesh. But the tinder was too dry, and all too soon the scorching heat forced him back.

The building was made of brick and the floor stone, and it was doubtful if it would actually catch fire. But he knew all too well that the flames were not what they had to fear most. Already the smoke was thickening, billowing out blackly, and making his eyes water. He knew they would both be long dead of heat and smoke before the flames did enough outward damage to bring anyone to investigate.

He hurried back to Alessia and carried her to the far side of the building, ignoring his weakened arm.

He removed her cloak to wrap it loosely about her face and mouth, hoping that would protect her for a little while.

She moaned a little as he bent over her, and then her eyes flickered open. They were sightless for a moment; then some recognition seemed to come into them, for she murmured, "It's you. I should have known you'd come."

"Shhh, sweetheart. Of course I did. What happened?"

"I don't know," she managed, her eyes closing weakly again. "I got your note and came . . . and then something hit me." She put up a shaky hand to the back of her head, and moaned even at her own touch. "Oh, God, my head . . . "

"Shhhh," he said reassuringly, pulling her hand away. "Just lie quietly and I'll get us out of here."

She exhaustedly closed her eyes again, for once as obedient as a child. Even in the glow from the fire her skin looked waxy pale and her face set. He guessed she was feeling too sick to care much what was happening, which was the only advantage he had discovered so far.

Certainly his blithe promise had been completely empty. He went back to the heavy doors, pounding on them and yelling, but he knew even as he did so that it was useless. Worse, it used up too much precious air, for he was already beginning to cough painfully.

What few windows the building possessed were too high for him to reach, and there was nothing he could use for a ladder. If he could get up there he might break one and manage to call for help, but he doubted if anyone would hear him. The coach house was not that far distant, but it was the dinner hour and few grooms would be about then.

The big heavy double doors seemed to offer his

only hope, and he tried throwing his weight against them. He succeeded only in bruising his already tender ribs and exhausting himself. He guessed that the doors were fastened by a heavy bar that would take a siege engine to break through.

Swearing at his own lingering weakness, he looked around for something to use as a seige engine, but nothing offered itself to his view. He was beginning to cough in earnest now, and ripped off his shirt to wrap around the lower part of his face to protect himself from the worst of the smoke.

It helped a little, though his eyes and lungs were burning painfully by then. He went back to check on Alessia, and found her curled feebly against the wall, her face buried in her cloak. She was in the furthest corner from the blaze, but it too was beginning to fill up with smoke, and he knew neither of them would last a great deal longer.

He forced his way back to the fire, now burning fiercely, feeling as if he were battling against a tangible wall of heat and smoke. His lungs were beginning to labor, which also did little good for his injured ribs, and he could feel the blistering heat on the exposed parts of his body. He wished desperately he had not stopped to change clothes, for he would have had several more garments, including a coat and waistcoat, to help protect him from the smoke and flames.

There was no choice, though. Using two dusty carriage rugs he found to protect his hands and arms, he began seizing burning material and throwing it against the heavy double doors. In the end he succeeded in building up quite a tidy little bonfire that began to rival the first for heat and intensity. But to make sure, he stayed feeding it until his lungs could stand it no longer, and he was beginning to reel from smoke inhalation and dizziness.

Then he retired to the corner where Alessia lay, to wait it out, hoping against hope that the wooden doors would burn through before they were both completely overcome.

He found her doubled up and coughing weakly. He took her tightly in his arms, protecting her as best he could, and saying foolishly, "Shhhh, sweetheart. Don't worry. It will be all right."

But inside he was wondering bleakly if they weren't both going to die there for his own mistakes in judgment. He knew then that he had never felt real fear in his life before, not even when he had stared down the muzzle of the pistol he had thought would kill him.

Once again he went back to check his own bonfire, and saw with satisfaction that the big doors were beginning to char. The conflagration was so great by now that he had to cover his face as he approached, and the room was thick with choking smoke, but things were still moving too slowly for his satisfaction. Like a madman he added more fuel to his fire, scarcely noticing how he was burned in the process, and only stopped to cough and put out the smoldering-hot spots as his protective blankets caught fire.

The doors, made of massive slabs, had still not begun to blaze, but they were blackened and beginning to weaken. He knew he could afford to waste no more time. He was himself feeling sick by then, and knew his strength, such as it was, was about gone.

Again like a madman he began to kick at the doors, scarcely noticing the scorching heat or the flames that almost engulfed him. Again and again they drove him back, but he knew if he didn't succeed they would both die anyway, and so he fought with a will and passion he had never given to any cause before, not fighting the Turks with the Greeks, or brigands in Corsica, or malaria in Egypt. The difference was, of course, that this time he was not fighting only for himself.

When the door at last gave, with a splintering crash and a great roar of sparks, it took him a moment to realize he had succeeded and to stop his wild onslaught. The first sweet, cool night air that reached him seemed like heaven.

18

Shielding both of them as much as possible with her cloak, Rhys staggered with Alessia in his arms through the splintered door and out into the cool night, forcing himself to go some way away before he at last collapsed with his burden. There he lay, gasping and coughing, too spent for anything else at the moment.

When he came to his senses, Alessia was lying on her side, retching weakly. Her garments were singed, her face blackened, and her eyes streaming. He had little doubt his own face was as unrecognizable.

He held her head until the worst of the retching was over, smoothing her hair back tenderly and murmuring wordless nonsense to her. At long last the sickness lessened and she turned over weakly and began to cry.

He was so overcome by this heretofore unexpected sign of weakness that he gathered her tightly into his arms, saying foolishly, "Hush, love. It's all right. You're safe now. Don't cry, sweetheart. Please don't cry. It's all right now."

They were found like that sometime later. The flames had at last attracted some attention, and men had poured out hurriedly, their napkins still tucked in their collars, reaching for the fire buckets as they came.

Rhys heard the questions and exclamations of horror only distantly, too exhausted by then even to feel relief. But he flatly refused to give up his hold on Alessia, and it was he who carried her unsteadily to the waiting carriage, then tumbled gratefully in after her.

The sensation they achieved at the dower house might, at any other time, have been amusing. Cousin Jane had called to confer with Alessia and been most annoyed at her absence. She had been making her displeasure felt to Clarissa when Rhys walked in, face and bare chest blackened and hair singed, with Alessia clasped tightly in his arms.

Clarissa gave a little scream and fainted dead on the spot, and even Jane fell back in horror. "Good God! What has happened? And who the devil are *you*?" she demanded weakly.

Rhys ignored her. "Miss Fielding's bedchamber," he snapped. "Which is it?"

Lady Fielding gaped at him, evidently torn between shock and wholly unworthy suspicion. "Have you run mad?"

Luckily Alessia's maid, Potton, appeared at that moment on the landing and answered quickly, "I'll show you, sir. This way."

He waited for no more, but carried Alessia up the stairs, Jane left speechless behind him.

If Potton had once disapproved of him, the fact was not in evidence at the moment. She took in the vision of her mistress singed and almost unrecognizable, overcome in his arms, composedly enough and directed him to her bedchamber at the top of the stairs. "I'll have the doctor sent for at once, sir. Though if I may say so," she added, looking him over, "you would appear to stand in as much need of a doctor as she does."

He glanced at himself in the mirror over Alessia's dresser and grimaced. His face was completely black, his hair and eyebrows singed, and he was becoming painfully aware of the burns across his arms and chest. It was little wonder Cousin Jane had thought the worst of him.

"I'm all right. Unfortunately your mistress had a blow on the head first, which accounts for her present sickness. But I don't think it's anything to worry about."

The doctor soon confirmed this comfortable diagnosis. Horsham had by then fetched Rhys a change of clothes, and as he cleaned himself up and slipped gratefully into them, he scarcely noticed that they were from his own wardrobe, not from the supposed Horsham's nephew's.

The doctor, when he came after tending to Alessia, looked him over and said bluntly, "Miss Fielding is suffering from nothing more than smoke inhalation and mild concussion. It's you I'm worried about. Her maid tells me you are only just recovered from another mishap, and you certainly look as if a mild wind would blow you over. For God's sake, man, sit down and stop playing the hero, for I can assure you I'm wholly unimpressed."

Rhys grinned, and willingly gave himself over to the other's bluff ministrations.

The doctor tut-tutted disapprovingly over the still-new scar in his side, anointed his many burns with salve, pronounced him lucky to have gotten off so lightly, and ordered him straight to bed. "And in case you have any foolish ideas in your head, I am instructed by the maid to tell you that Miss Fielding has been given a composer and will sleep for some hours yet, and Lady Fielding has gone home. I am leaving the same for you and have every intention of standing over you until you drink it."

He did so, remarking as Rhys drained the glass and grinningly handed it back, "Hmph! Some young men have far more nerve than sense. But I am also to tell you," he relented, his eyes beginning to twinkle a little, "that Potton will let you know as soon as her mistress wakens. Now, get some sleep yourself before you discover just how human you are."

Rhys gave up the unequal struggle and gratefully lay down on the cool, soft sheets. He was asleep almost before his head touched the pillows.

He woke, much later, to a hand on his arm, and Potton's voice saying calmly in his ear, "She's awake now, sir, and asking for you."

He struggled up, feeling groggy and aware by then of all his aches and pains, and demanded stupidly, "What time is it?"

"Almost morning, sir. But please keep your voice down. Miss Buel sleeps just across the passage."

He grinned and managed to rise, thinking the doctor had been more accurate than he knew. It seemed to him that every single part of his body ached, and his burns were beginning to make themselves painfully known.

He followed Potton to Alessia's bedchamber, and found her sitting up against her pillows, looking very white and small, her black hair unbound and spreading across her shoulders. At sight of him some of the anxiety left her face, and she said weakly, "Oh, thank God. I thought . . . I feared . . . Potton told me you were all right, but I couldn't believe—" Abruptly she surprised him very much by once more bursting into overwrought tears.

Any thought he might have had of maintaining a wise distance was defeated by her tears. He took her wordlessly into his arms, completely unaware when Potton discreetly withdrew from the room and closed the door behind her.

Alessia cried weakly on his shoulder for some

time, then at last hiccuped and made a feeble effort to pull herself together. "I'm sorry! I can't think what's come over me."

"Nor can I, unless it's the blow on the head and nearly being roasted alive," he countered, trying to revive her spirits. "But at least no one can complain it's boring living around me."

She laughed weakly at that. "No, not boring. But as usual, I fear you have taken the brunt of it. Oh, your poor face."

She put up a hand to touch his scorched face, her eyes filling unexpectedly with tears again. It was an innocent-enough gesture, had not the tears disarmed him completely. He groaned and caught her hand to his lips, saying foolishly, "Don't, my darling! I can't bear it! When I think . . ."

Then he broke off, too late aware of his mistake. The intimacy of the hour, their overwrought feelings—he should have waited to see her in the morning.

Her hand had frozen in his, both a question and an answer in her eyes, and he realized that both of them were trembling. For a moment longer he fought the temptation, knowing they were both in danger of being lost completely. He had no right to touch her—say anything more—for he had long ago chosen his road and there was no going back. He had learned that if he had learned nothing else in his long and varied life.

But her hair, black as a raven's wing, spread over his arms, and her white nightdress was soft and revealing. Even that he could have ignored had he not read the answer in her eyes, and a longing as great as his own in her face.

He groaned again and gave up the unequal struggle. "Oh, God, Angel! Don't look at me like that." Then he was kissing her frantically, her eyes, her hair, her throat. "I never meant . . . I had decided . . . especially when I saw you this afternoon and knew it was my fault. I don't think I've ever lived so long an hour in my life!"

"Stop talking nonsense and kiss me again!" Alessia managed, winding her arms tightly around his neck. "I was beginning to think you never would."

That drew a shaky laugh from him, and then he obeyed her. She kissed him back with a desperation he had not expected, and it defeated what little control he had left.

He knew it was madness, but at the moment he was beyond rational thought, and she was so sweet, so sweet. There was no fear in the lips she offered him, nor any doubt, and she gave herself with a generosity he had never known existed.

There was no telling how far it might have gone, for both of them were beyond rational thought, when Potton returned and interrupted them.

They broke apart, breathless and out of touch with reality, and he was not certain, either then or later, when he had belatedly gone back to his own room and resumed some sanity, whether to be glad or sorry.

He still had no idea when he came to see her the next morning.

He had gone straight back to the Horsham's cottage to avoid any more temptation, and it was late in the morning before he roused himself and managed to get his various aches and pains under sufficient control to rise and dress. Mrs. Horsham had been horrified at sight of him, and protested at him being out of bed, but he had kissed her on her sturdy cheek and ignored all her protestations.

He was admitted at the dower house without

question, though he had wondered whether he would be. He found Alessia lying on the sofa in the drawing room, fully dressed and with Clarissa fussing around her.

She was still pale, and there were dark smudges under her eyes. She had been lying with her eyes closed, but they opened immediately when he entered, as if she sensed his presence. She looked directly across at him, a certain shyness in her eyes, but none of the embarrassment he had been afraid he might find there.

But that was little enough comfort. "How are you feeling this morning?" he managed, knowing he was behaving stiffly but unable to act more normally.

She made a wry face. "As if my head's about to fall off, but the doctor assures me that's normal. How are you feeling?"

He managed to smile at her, feeling as if his scorched face would crack under the strain. "About the same. As if some fire dancers had been practicing on my body, in fact," he joked.

Clarissa was looking between them in growing outrage. "Alessia! Who is this man?" she demanded.

Rhys bestowed a look on her that had her suddenly red-faced. "I see what you mean," he murmured ruefully.

A hint of laughter came into Alessia's eyes. "Yes, but don't forget, she *means* well," she countered.

"*Alessia!* You are in no state to be receiving visitors. You know the doctor said you must keep quiet. You shouldn't even be out of bed yet."

He raised a questioning eyebrow at that. "That, at least, I suspect is true."

"Nonsense. I am persuaded you wouldn't have me languish upstairs and miss all the excitement over no more than a bruise on the head? At any rate, I am equally sure the doctor also told you you shouldn't remove the bandages you had on last night, but I noticed you haven't taken his advice either."

He smiled more naturally down into her eyes. "It seems we're a mad pair," he conceded ruefully.

"But then, that was established long ago," she acknowledged, equally gravely.

"*Alessia!*"

She glanced at Clarissa, then back to Rhys, and said without the slightest hesitation, "Clarissa, leave me now, please. I wish to be alone."

Rhys's mouth curved in silent appreciation, and Clarissa almost gaped at her. "But . . . but who *is* this man? What do you know about him? I am persuaded dear Lady Fielding would wish me to stay—especially as you are far from being yourself. In fact, I think I should send again for the doctor, for if you ask me, you are decidedly feverish."

"On the contrary, I am not in the least feverish. And while I am sure my cousin would indeed wish you to stay, I will remind you that Lady Fielding does not employ you—I do. At least for the time being. Now, please do as I say."

Clarissa had turned very red, and was now gobbling speechlessly at her. Rhys marchd smartly across, opened the door, and held it for her with exaggerated courtesy. "Miss Buel!" he prompted, and bowed politely.

She hung on for a momemt longer, then abruptly capitulated, and almost scuttled through the door. "Very well, then. I hope no one will say of me that I don't know when I'm not wanted!" she pronounced, very much on her dignity.

Alessia managed to hold her laughter until he had closed the door firmly behind her, then caught his mocking eye and doubled over with it.

"There," he said, coming lazily back into the room

and dusting off his hands. "Do you see how easy that was?"

She began to mop at her streaming eyes. "Yes, but only . . . only because . . ."

"No one will ever say of her she doesn't know when she's not wanted," he finished for her, enjoying her amusement.

"Oh, dear, don't! At any rate, I shouldn't laugh at her, poor thing."

"Why not? I find her eminently laughable."

She sobered slightly. "Yes, but she will go straight to Jane, I'm afraid, which will be far less laughable, believe me."

"But then, I have every confidence you are fully capable of dealing with Jane as well."

A smile crept back into her eyes. "If I am, I owe it all to you. You have been good for me, you know."

He came across and stood over her. "And is that designed to convince me it's not my fault you were nearly killed?"

She looked rueful. "You always were annoyingly able to read my mind. It is the one thing I dislike in you."

"Not that I am annoyingly stubborn as well, and dragged you straight into danger by my own refusal to take anything seriously? You are remarkably tolerant," he remarked lightly.

But there was a certain bleakness in his face, and her smile faltered a little. "I was afraid that was the way you would take it," she admitted. "But you might rather be berating me for having stirred up the hornet's nest, you know. Had I not gone to Crickfield, none of this would ever have happened, and you would probably be on your way back to Europe. In a way, I almost wish you were."

"So do I. You would then not now be lying with a bruise the size of an egg on the back of your head, and have almost been burned to death yesterday."

She half sat up, forgetting her headache. "Good God! You surely can't think it's because of that I wish none of it had happened? I assure you I am not so poor-spirited!"

His expression softened a little. "No, that at least I know. You have only now to try to reassure me that you positively enjoyed being hit upon the head and left to die in a burning building, and I will no doubt be thoroughly exonerated."

She smiled at that. "Well, no. But I have no one but myself to blame, you know, for you didn't want to believe it was your uncle who was involved. And I am very much afraid I've put your life in further danger, rather than solving anything. *That* is why I wished you'd already gone abroad, not my own safety."

Abruptly he came to kneel by her and take her hands in his painful ones. "And that is why I should do just that. Not for my own safety, but because I should never have allowed you to become involved."

"Very well. But what would you do if you need not worry about me?" she asked quietly.

He made a wry face and rose again to go and stare down into the small blaze in the fireplace. "I don't know," he admitted, his back to her. "I have never stood up for anything, or really wanted anything in my life—except my own freedom. But somehow, after yesterday, I have suddenly discovered that everything has changed. I might indeed have been prepared to turn my back on the mystery and do nothing more about it. But by cold-bloodedly drawing you in and risking your life as well, all for a handful of copper ore, my uncle has made a fatal mistake."

She seized on that at once. "The report was accurate, then?"

He shrugged and turned at last. "As far as it goes. There is still no guarantee, of course, even if the decision is made to sink a shaft—and the money found to finance it. As a motive for murder, I must admit that until yesterday I still thought it absurd."

Then he grimaced. "But there is still the fact that if I stay, if I choose to fight for it, I will only be putting you in further danger. How can I make that decision, especially for a thing I didn't even want two days ago?"

Her smile was oddly serene. "I think you have already made the decision, and it has less to do with me than you know. When it really came down to it, you couldn't choose to give in without a fight, just to keep me out of danger, any more than I could really wish you had gone away again. To do that is to live as I have lived for the last six months—and perhaps all of my life. Afraid to tilt with windmills, and as a result, only half-alive."

He stood looking at her, something like rueful admiration in his face. But their peace was at an end. The door flew open unexpectedly and Lady Fielding surged in, taking in the scene with scandalized eyes.

"*Alice!*" she cried in disbelief. "Have you taken leave of your senses?"

19

Alessia sighed and closed her eyes briefly. "Jane," she said flatly at last. "What a surprise."

Jane gave a harsh laugh. "It comes as no surprise to me to find you lost to all propriety! And this . . . this . . ." She regarded Rhys distastefully, and then frowned. "Don't I know this man? Good God! It's Horsham's nephew!"

Rhys was looking as if he was enjoying himself, and thankfully Alessia began to find her own sense of humor returning. "He is not Horsham's nephew. And I will remind you that while the Oaks is now yours, the dower house is mine. Neither you nor my cousin has any control over what I choose to do in it, contrary to what you seem to believe."

Jane's eyes had, if anything, taken on something of a look of triumph as she looked between them. "So it would seem. Henry always said there was nothing but your father in you, but then, Henry is a fool. I always knew your mother would come to the fore one day."

"And what the devil does she mean by that?" Rhys demanded, frowning.

"Alice knows exactly what I mean," Jane said deliberately. Then she smiled unpleasantly. "Or haven't you told him yet?"

"And why does she call you Alice?"

Alessia glanced at him, now that the moment had come, surprised at how calm she felt. "She finds my given name too . . . exotic for her taste. And she is referring to my Italian blood."

Jane's smile grew. "If that's what you care to call it. Henry has always chosen to believe the demure little act you put on, but no woman would be fooled for long by your looks. You look neither English nor respectable, as I've always said."

"*Much* less laughable," Rhys acknowledged grimly. "Shall I do the honors this time?"

"No. We both must learn to fight our own battles."

Jane had glanced between them during this exchange, and seemed to find it highly revealing. "I begin at last to see why the Season Henry insisted upon giving you, despite all my objections, was completely wasted. I should have known your taste would run to adventurers," she said spitefully.

A smile crept into Alessia's eyes at that. "Yes, I think it does," she admitted.

But Jane seemed to find her complete lack of anger or any defense of herself baffling. "Well, I have done all that I can to protect your reputation—with very little thanks, I might add," she pronounced at last. "When you have succeeded in ruining yourself, I only hope you won't come begging to me."

"No, Jane. You may be sure that is the last thing I would do."

Again Rhys had gone pointedly to the door and opened it, although this time his expression was far from amused. "Say good-bye," he instructed Alessia. "Lady Fielding is just going."

Jane gave him one comprehensive glance and swept from the room. But she could not resist a parting shot. "And don't expect Henry to stand by you either. He has found it difficult enough to excuse your birth without this. You may be quite sure he will be as disgusted as I am."

There was silence for a moment after she had

gone. "I somehow don't care for your cousin, Angel," Rhys remarked distastefully. "A most vulgar woman. What was that all about, by the way?"

She smiled and shrugged it away. "Her extreme vulgarity, I should imagine. You are very right about her."

"She is not only vulgar, and a pompous nodcock, but extremely paper-witted as well, if she takes such absurd exception to your Italian birth," he said wrathfully, warming to his theme. "How you have endured her even for six months, I don't know."

"No. But she is beneath notice. Let's not waste time talking about her. Let us instead discuss last night—or rather this morning. Or had you hoped I would have forgotten it?"

He halted and looked down at her, an oddly rueful expression coming into his eyes. "Perhaps I *had* hoped that," he acknowledged at last. "It would save me an apology, at least."

"But why should you feel the need to apologize—unless, of course, you didn't enjoy it?"

He gave a strangled laugh. "A novel viewpoint, but I should know by now that you're seldom predictable. Even so, I shouldn't have done it."

"Didn't you enjoy it, then?" she asked rather anxiously.

His amusement turned almost to annoyance. "For God's sake, Alessia. Even you should know you don't ask a man such a question. We were both overcome by the . . . hour and our recent harrowing experience. It meant nothing."

She blithely ignored that. "I must confess I enjoyed it very much—until we were so rudely interrupted. But if you didn't, naturally I wouldn't dream of asking you to repeat the experiment."

Rhys stood still, a half-smile on his mobile mouth

and a question beginning to form in his eyes. "You little devil! What are you up to? But very well." He leaned forward to press a chaste kiss on her forehead. "Does that satisfy you?"

She laughed up at him. "Only if it's the best you can do. I would have thought . . . friends could manage more than that. Or are you brave only at four A.M.?" she taunted him.

There was still a question in his eyes, and an unwonted wariness in his expression, but he hesitated, then shrugged and set his hands on her shoulders and kissed her lightly on the lips.

Except that the lips she raised to his were more than willing, and the chaste kiss he had obviously intended somehow changed and became a great deal more.

It was he who broke away first, and went to stand, his back to her and his breathing visibly uneven. "Dammit, Alessia!"

"You needn't worry," she said calmly, though her own color was a little heightened. "I take full responsibility. Did it never occur to you that a woman could be just as curious as a man? I wanted to know what it would be like to have you kiss me, and now I know."

"Good God, Alessia!" he cried, half-laughing again.

"Now you sound like Cousin Jane," she complained, teasing him. "I fear I have shocked you after all."

"Damn you, you little wretch! Of course I'm not shocked. But you can't go around saying such things. In case you don't know it, it's liable to get you in a great deal of trouble."

She was openly laughing now. "You mean that Cousin Jane might not approve? But I don't think I should use her as a model, do you? And naturally

I wouldn't say such things to just anyone—only my dearest friend."

His expression changed. "You have called me your friend from the beginning, but you will notice that I have never called you mine," he said deliberately. "But whether or not I enjoyed the little experiment you have just been conducting, it won't be repeated."

"That is a . . . shame," she said rather unsteadily. "For I enjoyed it immensely. And if I have called you my friend, it is only because you have never, until yesterday, shown by word or action that you thought of me as anything else. Frankly, I'll admit I was beginning to think there must be something wrong with me."

He was forced to laugh again. "I don't know why anything you do should surprise me by now. But if your vanity has been piqued, I will confess that I have wanted you from the moment I first woke to find you smiling down at me. But the . . . circumstances were somewhat unusual and I had not the right—neither then nor now—to do anything about it. Only an arch-rogue would take advantage of you under these circumstances. Believe me, we will soon both recover from our folly."

"You mean, I expect," she said even more calmly, "that I cannot compete with your freedom and the lure of far-off places. It's all right. I don't blame you for that."

He swore. "No, that is not what I meant. When I am in your presence I tend to forget everything else, including my own name. Haven't you guessed that by now? But it's madness. It will pass. It must."

"I must take your word for it. I only know that I never before knew why women did such foolish things for love. Now I do. And I'm not sure I want it to pass."

He almost groaned. "Oh, God, you little fool! You indeed know little of men if you think you're not playing with fire and liable to get burned. My intentions are honorable in this case, but I have nothing to offer you, and no promises for the future. You should know that better than anyone."

"But I want no promises from you," she said simply, all her doubts dropping away. "Nothing you can't keep or will come later to regret. And I have discovered that I quite badly want to get burned."

The humor slowly disappeared from his eyes, and for once he appeared shaken. "My dear, don't!" he said in a low voice, as if against his will. "You don't know what you're saying."

But she had come too far to lose her courage now. "At least do me the courtesy of not treating me as a child. I know exactly what I'm saying. I am six-and-twenty. You heard Jane. The chances are not high I shall ever marry."

"Jane is a fool," he interrupted impatiently, "and extremely jealous of you to boot. Don't talk such nonsense."

"No . . ." She spoke with the simplicity of utter conviction. "I used to think I might eventually find a man I was willing to spend the rest of my life with—someone uncluttered by the usual prejudices and dictates of society. But I should have known that when I did, he would be too unconventional to want what other men want."

He turned away, lacking the courage to face what she was telling him. "Angel," he said with difficulty, "I am more like other men than you know. Don't you think if I could offer you anything—anything at all—I would be down on my knees before you?"

"Don't! I promise this is not a plot to extort an offer of marriage from you. I am only trying to explain why I am doing what I am."

"You don't have to explain!" he said quickly. "In fact this whole conversation is becoming absurd. You talk as if you are at your last prayers. You have your whole life still before you."

"Yes, but before you say what you are so obviously thinking—that I should go to Bath, or even London, in seach of a husband—I should perhaps tell you that I had a Season in London when I was twenty. And Jane was quite right, I'm afraid. It was an unmitigated disaster."

"Come, I find that hard to believe."

"Perhaps I should say, then, that I disliked London as much as it seemed to dislike me. Jane is not the only one to regard me as too foreign in my looks to be generally appreciated. Worse, I was known to be that most unfeminine of all creatures, an intellectual woman. Perhaps not surprisingly, I was also ill-at-ease and lacked either the fortune or the beauty to overcome my own drawbacks. Men fled from me in droves. During the whole Season I received only one offer, and that was from a man more than old enough to be my father, who only wished to marry me to acquire a glorified governess for his numerous daughters."

He had listened to this remarkable speech with growing impatience. "I can see that it must have been a painful time, but it is ridiculous to decide your future on the basis of one unfortunate Season and a gaggle of fools you cared nothing about. If all the eligible bachelors of that year were blind, it doesn't follow that every man is."

She smiled. "Perhaps not. There are . . . other reasons that figure into it that I don't wish to go into at present. But I'm not telling you this to invoke your sympathy or to invite an argument. I'm telling you as a simple fact that I sincerely doubt that I shall ever marry. But I still have a . . . a desire to know what I may be missing. Is that so unnatural?"

He took her hand and held it tightly between both his own. "It is not in the least unnatural, although you are the first woman I've ever met—at least of your class—who was honest enough to confess it."

She grimaced. "Perhaps Jane is right after all, then."

"Jane is a harpy. Undoubtedly she, like most women, would prefer to pretend she is overpowered, so that she may escape the inevitable responsibility and regrets for her actions later. But however natural your feelings may be, the situation is far from being natural. And what you are asking—"

She refused to let him finish. "Perhaps I should make it perfectly clear to both of us what I am asking before you say any more. I . . . like you better than any man I've ever met. No!" as he started to speak again. "You needn't worry. I assure you I cherish no illusions about your feelings for me, or the possibility of any permanent arrangement between us. I know you have no desire to settle down, and that your own future is far from secure. I have told you that this is not some devious attempt to force you into matrimony against your will."

He raised her hand to his lips and kissed it gently. "That, at least, I know, Angel," he said ruefully.

"Good. I . . . I wanted to get that clear from the outset. I am financially independent, and though not particularly happy at the moment, I have no need of a husband either for security or for the sake of appearances. And since in twenty-six years I have never met the man who could tempt me to give up my freedom, I now doubt that I ever will. I am telling you all this so you can see I have thought it all out carefully, and that I know what I'm doing."

This time he made no attempt to interrupt her,

his eyes fixed oddly on her face, an expression in them she could not read. She discovered she wished quite desperately she could know what he was thinking, and had never regretted his elusiveness more.

But in the absence of any hint from him, she had no choice but to go on. "I fear this is harder than I ever imagined it would be! But then, I hadn't envisioned exactly how . . . brazen it would sound, put into words. But the point is, I know my own mind and I am of age. And . . . and I see no reason why, simply because I choose never to marry, I should deprive myself of what every woman has a right to know."

Still he said nothing. She said desperately, "I must admit I had expected more help from you. Must I put it in words of one syllable for you? I am quite willing—indeed anxious—to become your mistress."

20

Still Alessia found she could not read his expression. He had retained her hand, but though his hold on it remained light and undemanding, she thought there was a bleakness in his face that she had never seen before.

For a moment she feared she had indeed offended him, but did not know what else she could have done. Before last night he had given no indication he would ever make a move toward her, and he had now told her why. But since she was grasping at her one chance at happiness—however temporary—she could not afford to let his scruples stand in her way.

Then at last he said almost harshly, "I won't insult you by saying you can't know your own mind or engage in the usual politely veiled terms that pass for frankness between the sexes. But I think there is at least one thing you haven't considered. What if you should become pregnant?"

She actually smiled. "Then I would be very glad. It would give me the incentive I seem to need to leave this district, and I could easily establish myself as a widow somewhere else, you know. At any rate, you needn't worry. I have told you I will not hold you to any obligations or responsibilities. Whatever should become of such a . . . a liaison would be my own problem entirely."

"Generous of you!" he snapped.

She frowned, realizing she had never seen him look quite that way before. She still could not read his mood to tell whether he was shocked, angry, amused, or repelled by her suggestion, but the easygoing companion of the last few weeks was completely gone now.

"*Are* you shocked or angry with me?" she asked at last.

His mobile mouth twisted, and for a moment he looked her familiar friend again. "Not . . . angry, Angel. And I would be less than human if I said your offer wasn't tempting. But despite your six-and-twenty years, I think you have very little experience of the world—particularly of what you would be letting yourself in for. And while I am no saint, I would have to be a villain indeed to take my pleasure now and leave you to cope with the consequences."

"I . . . see. And if I said I was more than willing to take that risk?"

He hesitated, then shook his head. "Even if you were willing, I fear I'm not."

Pride made her blink back the threatened tears and smile steadily up at him. "I see. I am to be denied my one chance to be a woman in order to suit your pride. Is that it?"

"If you must put it that way. I care for you too deeply to take what you so sweetly offer and then leave you in the lurch. And you are right that my future has no place in it at the moment for anyone else. Under the circumstances, the chances are not high that I will even be alive six months from now. I . . ." Then he shook his head, as if stopping himself from saying more, and merely waited.

At last she was sufficiently in control of herself to say with an appearance at least of calm, "It seems we are at an impasse. Will you at least stay on at the Horshams? You are not sufficiently—"

"No," he said gently, and left it at that.

"I . . . see. You're probably right."

"No, I don't think you see at all. But it is no doubt better that way. Will you be all right with your cousin?"

"Yes, of course." Then she smiled more naturally. "I told her the truth, you know. She really has no power over me. You taught me that. She is annoyed at the moment, but her pride is too great to enable her to break publicly with me."

"And Miss Buel?"

She shrugged. "I must confess I care little one way or the other. Tongues would wag if I lived here without a chaperone, but they have always wagged anyway. And I must confess it would be a comfort to be rid of her. I'm sure Jane will be more than glad to take her in and keep her occupied."

"Well, then."

She thought he seemed eager to go, and knew a fresh pang. But she had done all she could, and been rejected. "So it seems our adventure is finally over," she managed at last. "And you? Will you be going back abroad immediately?"

"Good God," he said, sounding surprised. "I'm not going abroad. I'm going to Crickfield, of course."

With that Alessia had to be content. Her pride should have been in tatters at her feet, but she found that once she had recovered from her earlier disappointment, oddly enough that did not seem to be the case. In fact she felt oddly serene, as if she were waiting for something, though she would not put a name to what that was.

Not even Jane could get through to her any longer. As she had predicted, Jane did not dare risk an open breach, but Alessia had to endure a painful episode with Henry.

He looked extremely uncomfortable, and even

half-ashamed of himself. Alessia knew he had been genuinely fond of her when they were children and that he took his duties as head of the household seriously, and so found she could not be angry with him.

She endured as many of his stumbling questions and protestations as she cared to, then interrupted him gently. "Henry, whatever Jane may have convinced you of, you have no control over me, either morally or legally. You don't even have the right to remove me from the dower house, but if you wish me to go, I will. Do you?"

He looked shocked at that. She guessed that had Jane not forced the issue, he would never have dared to broach the subject at all with her, and now he seemed completely torn. "No, no. Good heavens, no! Jane . . . well, she is an amazingly strong woman. Have to admire her for that. But not even she . . . No, no! I would never agree to that. You're my cousin, after all, and Uncle William left you to my care. At any rate, the place is yours. I hope you know I would never dream of interfering with that."

She was touched, and even forbore to point out to him that her father had certainly not left her in his care. He took his leave soon after, plainly at a loss, and she feared he was in for a stormy session with his wife.

Whatever the outcome of that meeting between husband and wife, Jane soon resumed her former manner toward Alessia, at least outwardly. There was a new, unpleasant knowledge in her eyes when they rested on her that Alessia found extremely annoying, but she told herself that she was lucky if that were the only repercussion she had to deal with, and tried to ignore it.

The interview with Clarissa proved to be less satisfying, and in the end far more painful, however.

Alessia had determined to harden her heart against her companion, and was therefore astonished when Clarissa came to her and quite humbly apologized.

"I can only hope that nothing I may have said or done has in any way . . . offended you or affected your confidence in me," she said awkwardly, twisting her handkerchief between tortured fingers. "If . . . if I exceeded my place this morning, I must beg your pardon."

Alessia's heart sank. She had cravenly hoped Clarissa would be too shocked and angry to want to remain, and this new meekness surprised and disarmed a good deal of her anger.

As if reading her thoughts, Clarissa added miserably, "I know that you never wished for a companion in the first place. But I have discovered that I have been oddly happy here. If I have seemed to be disloyal or to put myself too far forward, I can only promise that it will never happen again, and hope that you will manage to overlook it."

Alessia almost groaned. She was in no mood to soothe Clarissa's wounded sensibilities, and was indeed tempted to choose that way to be rid of her once and for all. But though she was frequently impatient with the older woman, she found she could not deliberately wound her, or harden her heart to a legitimate apology.

At any rate, she supposed she should be glad, for to have deliberately set out to shock the neighborhood by openly dismissing her companion would have done neither of them much good.

So she accepted Clarissa's apologies, and her subsequent overly morbid anxiety not to offend with resignation. And one piece of good had come out of it, at least. If Clarissa had not quite broken with Jane, she was careful after that to speak her name less often in Alessia's hearing, and once or twice was even heard to utter a mild criticism against her. It began to seem they might someday reach a compromise and live together in something approaching peace.

With Jane, of course, it was not so easy. She might not dare risk an open breach, but she managed to make her disapproval felt in a dozen minor ways. Nor in such a restricted neighborhood was it possible for Alessia to avoid her. And whenever they met, Jane seemed to take delight in needling Alessia. She also frequently was to be found watching her, an unpleasant expression on her face, as if seeking some crack in her armor.

Once, when they happened to have been left alone together for a few moments at a friend's house, Jane inquired maliciously, "And have you heard from your friend since he left?"

Alessia's heart had begun to beat a little fast, but she made herself look up calmly. "Which friend?"

"Don't play games with me! The man you were carrying on with so scandalously right under our very noses! Henry may have had the wool pulled over his eyes, but I assure you I'm not so easily fooled."

Alessia almost smiled. "No. I haven't heard from him," she admitted.

Jane observed her, almost as if perplexed by something. "That at least I can believe! It's obvious he took advantage of what was so clearly offered, but once he had finished with you, he couldn't wait to be gone! The thing I can't figure out is why you still look so disgustingly self-satisfied. Have you no pride whatsoever?"

Alessia did laugh then. "Perhaps I haven't. At least not the kind of pride that seems to think love a war to be won or lost. There must indeed be more of my mother in me than I had thought, as you like to point out. Whatever her background might have been, I think she knew how to love and be loved in return. If I have inherited that from her, I shall be grateful."

Jane rose as if she couldn't sit still any longer. "That is disgusting!" she snapped. "If I had my way, women like you would be—"

Then she broke off, seeming to realize she had gone too far.

But Alessia completed the sentence for her. "Women like me should be whipped at the cart tail?" she asked in amusement. "Is that what you were about to say? Perhaps so. But I would choose that any day over the joyless life you must live."

Even Jane flushed darkly, for once jarred from her usual massive self-possession. "I don't understand you at all!" she railed. "He has abandoned you! Why should you still defend him and look so happy? *Why?*"

But luckily the others came back into the room then and Alessia was spared an answer. She was surprised to have discovered that far from despising Jane any longer, she deeply pitied her.

Even so, out of both pride and a certain misguided vanity, she had no intention of admitting that Rhys had not seduced and then abandoned her, but had rejected her most unwomanly offer out of hand.

That made her laugh to herself, for the truth would undoubtedly have shocked Jane even more profoundly. At any rate, now that Alessia came to think of it, there was nothing in the least unwomanly in her offer. In fact she had never felt more like a woman than at that moment.

But Jane was right. On the surface at least, Rhys

had abandoned her. Alessia knew she should be feeling hideously embarrassed and humiliated. But she had told Jane the truth when she said there must be far more of her mother's heritage in her than she had ever suspected.

Certainly her offer had not been made either lightly or impulsively. Since Rhys had first come into her life, she had reflected endlessly on the future and what it held for her. She had never deluded herself that he could offer her any permanance, for he had spent his life avoiding ties and responsibilities. To ask him to change for her sake would be to lose him in the end more surely than any number of miles separating them could do.

But she had discovered she was far from resigned to never having known his passion or tenderness; or, his hunger having been satisfied, his lazy appreciation afterward. She thought he would be a tender lover, both caring and generous, and had known for weeks now that whatever the reason or cost, no other man would do for her.

Well, she had dared to offer herself and been rejected. As Jane obviously thought, she should have been too embarrassed to ever lift up her head again.

Instead she felt oddly free. She need no longer pretend with him what her feelings were, or fear to act upon them. She did not even feel any particular shame. He had refused her, but it seemed that he had left her pride intact after all.

And as Jane had somehow recognized, she found it impossible to consider it over between them. She was indeed waiting for something, even she hardly knew what. She had not heard a single word from him since he had left. He might even now be halfway to Timbuktu. Or dead.

But somehow her heart would accept neither.
And so she waited and hoped, oddly content for the moment, and hardly daring to put a name to what it was she was waiting for.

21

Almost a fortnight after Rhys had left, Alessia received unexpected news in the form of a visit from Mr. Owen Fitzwarren.

He looked slightly ill-at-ease as he came in. "I beg your pardon, Miss Fielding, I had no right to presume, but—"

Alessia had risen at his unexpected entrance, her heart suddenly in her throat and her knees oddly weak. "Don't apologize, Mr. Fitzwarren. Only tell me—is Rhys . . . ?"

He came contritely toward her, compassion warming his voice. "No, no! Nothing to alarm you so. I didn't mean to frighten you."

She still felt a little faint, proving to herself what a lie she had lived with for the last few weeks. But she said merely, "Then, pray sit down and tell me why you have come."

He did so, but seemed to find it hard to come to the point. "I'm not sure I can," he confessed ruefully. "The truth is, I fear my cousin may be in danger, and I can't seem to get through to him. I was hoping perhaps you could talk some sense into him."

She waited for no more. "Only let me get my cloak and leave a note for my companion and I'll be ready."

He rose gratefully. "Bless you. I know I have no right to ask, but . . . well, thank you."

When she returned some ten minutes later, he took her cloak from her and put it around her shoulders and then escorted her out to his waiting phaeton.

He apologized for the open carriage as well, explaining that he had not wanted to arouse suspicion by having a traveling coach brought round. In addition, he had left on something of the spur of the moment. "Though I suspect Rhys will have my hide when he learns I dragged you in," he confessed, helping her in and tucking the carriage rug securely around her.

"Please—I have heard nothing since he left here," she said anxiously. "He did come to Crickfield, then?"

Again he hesitated. "You must know this is not easy for me, Miss Fielding," he said at last. "Oh, yes, he came. I am quite fond of my cousin, Miss Fielding, but perhaps you will understand when I say his return was not an unalloyed pleasure," he added dryly.

"You knew nothing, then?"

"Nothing. Nor did I find it an easy topic to discuss. One does not readily accept that one's father may be a murderer," he said even more bitterly.

Instinctively she put out a gloved hand to cover his on the reins. "I know. It sounds inadequate to say I'm sorry. Is it true, then?"

He gratefully returned the pressure. "Oh, yes. I fear my father was finally moved to admit it to me, when faced with all the evidence."

"I'm sorry," she said inadequately again. "You knew nothing of possible copper under Crickfield, then?"

He smiled without humor. "Unhappily enough, I fear it was I who gave my father the idea in the first place, even before my uncle died. Needless to say, I am sorry now the cursed copper was ever discovered. But I had no way of knowing then, of course, that my father was in rather serious financial straits, or what lengths he might go to to save himself."

Again he hesitated. "I have no wish to defend my father, Miss Fielding, but . . . well, pride has always been his chief fault. I fear he could not face financial ruin. He would, quite literally, rather die first. And my cousin is not entirely blameless in all this, you know. I believe it must have seemed a harmless-enough plot in the beginning. It was only when my cousin returned unexpectedly that things began to get out of hand."

"Then you believe your father had nothing to do with his brother's death?" she asked curiously.

He appeared startled at the suggestion. "Oh, no. Good God, no! He did take it upon himself to exaggerate his devotion during those last months, and admittedly preyed upon my uncle's resentment on my cousin's continued absence. But the will was genuine enough, and my uncle's death long overdue, believe me. At least I need have no guilt over that."

She was not herself so sure, but saw no point in forcing the issue when he was already so obviously distressed. "And then Rhys came home," she prompted when he remained silent for a moment.

He seemed to stir himself to continue, though it was obvious he would rather not. "Yes. Until then I believe my father had managed to justify his actions by telling himself my cousin didn't deserve such a windfall and that he himself was responsible for the discovery of copper on Crickfield in the first place. His conscience at that point must have been fairly clear. He really is not a complete monster, you know."

Again she waited patiently, knowing it would do no good to comment.

Then he shrugged. "And then he got word from our solicitor that my cousin had returned home unexpectedly and he had to face seeing it perhaps all come to nothing. He was understandably enraged."

"But why? You've said yourself Lord Walter was left the property. Rhys could be no threat to him."

"Perhaps not, but again, it's easy to follow his thinking. He is not, I'm glad to say, an experienced plotter. He feared that Rhys might make a claim of undue influence, especially once the truth about the copper came out. I really think he felt he had gone too far to turn back by then."

She thought Owen was clutching at straws, but had no idea what she herself might have done had it been her own father. "But now you say your father has admitted his guilt? How, then, can Rhys be in any further danger?"

"I'm afraid I now come to what is even more difficult for me to discuss, Miss Fielding. He has admitted it, yes, but only to me. And the fact does remain that he owns Crickfield legally."

"But surely—"

"Yes, I know. It seems monstrous. It *is* monstrous. But the fact also remains that my cousin is, thankfully and in large part due to you, still alive. At present the most my father could be charged with is attempted murder, and since it's unlikely the men whom he hired to kill my cousin could be found, or made to testify, I doubt anything could ever be proved."

"But I saw one of them myself!" she protested.

"Yes, so my cousin told me. Unfortunately, I doubt he will ever be heard from again. You do see the dilemma, don't you?"

She shivered a little, finding his pragmatic logic little to her liking. "In other words, your father is likely to get away with it," she concluded, unable to keep the bitterness out of her voice.

He heard it, and smiled ruefully. "I sympathize with your feelings, Miss Fielding, believe me I do. But you must understand that neither my cousin nor I really desire such a scandal to become public. And my father will not be getting away unscathed, believe me. He has been much chastened by having it all come to light. For a man of his pride, that has not been easy. In addition he has consented—under much pressure from me—to share any proceeds from possible mining operations with my cousin. And I know what you're thinking! But keep in mind that my uncle legitimately left the estate to him and that my cousin never evinced the slightest interest in owning it. It is far more than a court of law would make him do, believe me. My father, of course, would be socially ruined, which is how I have been able to persuade him to be reasonable, but legally my cousin is not entitled to anything."

She was exceedingly angry at such a cynical viewpoint, but had to make herself remain calm. "Very well. And what is Rhys to do in return?"

He glanced at her in surprise.

"You said you wanted my help," she offered dryly in explanation. "Obviously to persuade him to do something he's not inclined to do."

"Ah, you're very quick," he said with a smile. "My cousin has merely to guarantee to return abroad—which is, after all, what he wanted in the first place. And again I can guess what you're thinking. But believe me, Miss Fielding, I have struggled with this for weeks now, and I'm convinced it's the best answer for everyone—at least during my father's lifetime. After that . . . well, I think I need hardly tell you that I will turn Crickfield over to Rhys without delay."

"I'm glad to hear it. But your cousin is obviously resisting. Is that right?"

"Yes. He always was ridiculously stubborn. Only this time he may be risking his life."

She said evenly, "I think you had better be a little more explicit, Mr. Fitzwarren. What exactly do you mean?"

"Oh, God! I'm sorry, but you can have little understanding, Miss Fielding, of how galling this is! If you must have it in plain words, I am very much afraid that my father has little left to lose. My cousin's life may be in more danger now than before. But I can't make him see that half of a much-enriched loaf is better than none at all. I am hoping you may be able to help me convince him."

She felt a chill that had little to do with the evening breeze, and wondered if he could know what he was asking of her. But he probably did. If he had been able to keep few secrets from her, she doubted she had kept many more from him. She said after a moment, "I see. Let us have all our cards on the table, if you please, Mr. Fitzwarren. You think I am an . . . obstacle of some sort."

He had the grace to look sheepish. "I'm sorry. I have no wish to pry. But I do know my cousin feels he owes some . . . duty to you. It may literally cost him his life, however, and I can't think you'd want that."

"And you don't think it strange that you are protecting your father even under these extreme circumstances?" she asked with a certain bitterness.

"I am protecting my cousin, Miss Fielding," he countered, with the first flash of anger she had yet seen. "I will admit my emotions are hardly undivided, but I really am trying to do the best for everyone."

She shrugged. "At any rate, I fear you are mistaken. Your cousin owes me no allegiance. We parted with no promises made on either side."

"Then you will try to make him see sense and leave England?" he asked eagerly.

It was her turn to smile without humor. "I make no promises. But I have as little desire to see him dead as you have. It would seem I have no other choice."

He looked relieved, and smiled back at her with a trace of his cousin's charm. "Thank you! I think I know how much that cost you. But I knew from the first time we met that you were a sensible woman."

He seemed to know not to press it any further, for the conversation lapsed between them after that.

She was grateful for the silence. She did not blame Owen, however cold-blooded he might appear. He could be finding little pleasure in any of it, and was simply trying to make the best of an impossible situation.

Nevertheless, she found little to like in his solution, however practical. Lord Walter was to remain, full of honors and wealth, while Rhys was once again the outcast. Even had her own emotions not been so closely involved, she still would have found it unjust.

But she knew that Owen was also right, and that so long as his uncle was alive, Rhys would always be in danger in England. Owen had made no mention of that last attempt on both of them, but Lord Walter must think himself relatively safe now. Once things had settled down a little, a convenient accident could always easily be arranged. And Owen, no matter what the state of his conscience, might be persuaded to keep silent in the interests of loyalty and family honor. Wasn't he already more or less apologizing and excusing his father's actions?

And so she returned to Crickfield one last time, in a very different state of mind, for she could see no happy ending for anyone.

Owen left her in a little glade by the side of the drive, saying apologetically, "I think it would be best if you don't come to the house. I'll bring Rhys to you. I shouldn't be gone above fifteen minutes, but you won't be cold, will you?"

She denied it, seeing no point in admitting that she feared she would be cold for the rest of her life. And the little glade was pleasant enough, with the sun shining through the leaves in dappled patterns and a delightful brook running nearby.

Nonetheless she shivered when he had gone, both longing for and dreading the coming interview. She had desperately wanted to see Rhys again, but she had never envisioned quite these circumstances.

Slightly more than ten minutes had passed, during which she had paced the little glade, struggling against the inevitable, when she at last heard the phaeton returning. Even then it was too soon, and she cravenly longed to put off the moment a little longer when she must send him away for good.

But there was no time. The carriage halted and she heard Rhys's voice, light and curious. "What the devil are you being so mysterious about, you fool? If this is some kind of trick, I warn you I'll pay you back. I haven't forgotten, even if you have, the time you lured me into the attics when we were boys, and had several of the stable lads dressed up in sheets to scare me."

She heard Owen laugh and make some disclaimer, and was suddenly unworthily jealous of the obvious friendship between them. But she knew she must begin to accustom herself to a lifetime of such regrets.

As Rhys entered the little glade, still laughing, she calmly stepped forward to meet him.

22

Luckily he was alone. When he recognized her he stood very still, and she faltered, suddenly horribly uncertain. If she saw reluctance, or even worse, embarrassment, in his face, she would know without a doubt that the dream was over, and she was suddenly not sure she could bear it.

Then he moved swiftly toward her, grasping her hands tightly in his own and saying in a husky voice, "Angel! What are you doing here?"

She still was uncertain and oddly tongue-tied. "I . . . Your cousin brought me to try to talk some sense into you."

His expression remained unreadable, but he looked slightly amused at that for some reason. "I see. And did you come for the same reason?" he asked quietly.

She made herself meet his eyes and say calmly, "Yes. Your cousin seems to think you are still in danger, and I fear he's right. At any rate, you know you never meant to stay in England. I want you to go now, before it's too late."

His hands tightened on her own, almost unconsciously. "Do you? But you see, I fear I am in danger almost anywhere I go," he remarked conversationally. "For I have discovered I will never be free again."

Her heart gave a great leap at the possible meaning of his words, and almost immediately plummeted again. "Free . . . of what?" she managed in a low voice.

He gave his attractive crooked grin. "Of a black-haired angel who has somehow managed to clip my wings. Wherever I go from now on I fear I will take her image with me. Did you really think I could walk away so easily, you little fool?"

She closed her eyes weakly and clung to his hands for support. "No," she whispered at last. "No more than I could be free of you. But I promised myself I would never tie you down, and I meant it. You have spent your life running away from responsibility."

"I have spent my life running away from my father's demented dreams," he corrected. "And I won't deny I've enjoyed the last six years. But to face another six—or a lifetime—without you seems not freedom any longer, but banishment. Can you understand that, sweetheart?"

She dared to open her eyes, hope clamoring in her heart and tears starting in her eyes. "Yes, for I feel the same," she admitted shakily. "But I won't be responsible for your death, any more than I would for your loss of freedom. Your cousin is right. You must go away."

He hesitated oddly. Then he smiled faintly. "My cousin. Yes. My cousin is almost always right, I fear. But don't cry, Angel. Let me take you home, and we'll discuss it later. How did you manage to slip away from the dragon, by the way?"

She laughed and dabbed foolishly at her tears, ashamed of her earlier melodrama. "I left a note for her. She is much less of a dragon these days. I even have hope we may one day become friends."

"And Jane?" he teased. "Do you have similar hopes for her?"

"No. Jane and I have temporarily declared a truce. She thinks, by the way," she admitted ruefully, "that I am a fool for not having known when I was rejected."

Once more his hands tightened possessively. "And did you know you hadn't been rejected?" he asked lazily. "Perhaps you are finally learning to value yourself properly after all."

"And you are as outrageous as ever!" she countered, striving for some much-needed lightness. "But if I knew you hadn't abandoned me, it is only because I seem to have as little sense as you. Your cousin is far more practical."

"Yes, my cousin," he said once more, and left it at that. "Did he bring you in the phaeton? I'm afraid it will be dark before I can get you home again, and you may jeopardize this new understanding with Clarissa. But you shouldn't be too cold."

He had put an arm around her and begun to walk her toward the road. They had gone very few steps when Owen appeared, eyeing them questioningly. "Well? Is everything settled?" he asked anxiously.

Rhys had resumed his bland mask. "I am escorting Miss Fielding home again," he said calmly.

"And what does that mean? Did she manage to convince you how dangerous it would be to stay?"

"Let us just say she convinced me you both believe so," said Rhys noncommittally.

Owen once more looked between them. "Look," he said. "I can see I underestimated what there is between you. But you will have enough money to take her with you if you choose. You know you can trust me to see that Father lives up to his bargain."

"Can I? But then Miss Fielding might have something to say about that."

"Good God, it's obvious she's head over heels in love with you! I'm sorry, but things have gone too far to balk at a little plain speaking now. Take her with you, if you must. After all, she has little room to object. I mean, it's not as if anyone else is likely to have her."

Rhys stilled, and Alessia watched the coming scene with an odd sense of detachment. Now that the thing she had dreaded for so long was finally happening, it was as if it were happening to someone else, not her.

"And what the devil do you mean by that?" demanded Rhys in a hard voice.

Owen once more looked between them. "Nothing. I'm sorry I mentioned it," he said unwillingly. "I just naturally assumed that she must have told you."

"Why don't you tell me instead?" Both seemed to have forgotten her.

"Look, I'm sorry I said anything."

"But you have. Now why don't you finish it?"

Owen seemed suddenly to lose his temper. "Don't play any of your silly games at a time like this! Very well, if she won't tell you, I will. Miss Fielding should be grateful enough to accept your . . . proposition, because she knows as well as I do she's unlikely to receive a more advantageous offer. Everyone knows her mother was a common prostitute, so she can really have little room to quibble at the life you're offering her."

Alessia felt oddly glad now that it was out. She was even able to say calmly, as Rhys growled something and started violently toward his cousin, "No, Rhys! Leave him alone!"

He stopped, for once obviously angry and uncertain. "Why? It's not true, is it?"

"No, it's not true. But it's near enough the truth that it scarcely matters."

As Owen gave an unkind laugh, she said more

quietly, "I'm sorry I didn't tell you before. And that you have to hear it under such circumstances. But I did try to tell you that I'm unlikely to receive any other offers."

He had halted, his eyes fixed now on her face in painful intensity. "Then why don't you tell me now?" he suggested gently at last.

She swallowed, even now finding it strangely hard to put into words. "Very well. My mother was not . . . a common prostitute, but she was a famous actress in Italy. She had also had an . . . affair with another man before my father. I make no apologies for her. She evidently had considerable talent, and came from an extremely poor family. She did what she had to in order to survive. My father, I'm thankful to say, fell almost instantly in love with her and had the sense to care more for her future than her past. But so long as she lived, and knowing the difficulties, he chose to remain in Italy. He brought me back to England only after she died."

Then she lifted her head. "But it was too much to expect he could keep it a complete secret. I have known the truth since I was eight, and have grown used to its effect on others. As you heard, my cousin Jane seems to think my mother's heritage will one day manifest itself in me, and I daresay she is not alone in that opinion. Your cousin seems to join her."

"Why didn't you tell me?" he asked at last.

"Because at first I was ashamed to have you know. And afterward I didn't want to use it as a tool against you. Can you understand that? Had you known the truth, you would have been disgusted—as your cousin so plainly is—or have felt the need to prove it didn't matter by making commitments I wasn't sure you wanted to make to me. And either way would have been equally impossible."

"My dear—"

She smiled and held up her hand. "No, don't say anything yet. I am still afraid of forcing the issue, of burdening you with unwanted baggage, only to find out, too late, that you travel best alone and unencumbered after all. But it seems I have not the luxury of such doubts now. If you . . . want me, I will willingly accompany you wherever you choose to go. I do think your cousin is right, and you will never be safe in England so long as your uncle is alive."

His grip tightened on her hand, but he said merely, "Then let me drive you home and we will discuss it later."

"I'm afraid that won't be possible," Owen said.

Alessia looked up to discover in astonishment that Owen had removed a pistol from his pocket and was now calmly pointing it at her. "That was a very touching scene, but I'm afraid neither of you will be going anywhere," he added in amusement.

She stiffened, and felt Rhys's warning pressure. "So it was you after all?" he inquired matter-of-factly.

Owen laughed. "I wondered if you suspected. Father is incapable of planning such an elaborate scheme, but I wasn't sure you knew it. He was willing enough to go along with it—but then, I haven't told him about the attempt at murder. He has the same antiquated notions about honor that your father did. And they are about as profitable, I regret to say. I prefer something a little more practical than spending my life congratulating myself on having been born a Fitzwarren."

"Yes, so I began to suspect," remarked Rhys conversationally.

"Did you? That was bright of you. But somewhat belated. Imagine my surprise when you appeared and began to confide in me so touchingly. In fact it was sometimes hard to keep from laughing. At first I even had some notion I might be able to persuade you to return abroad and keep your mouth shut, for I knew you had never wanted Crickfield. But unfortunately, I had reckoned without the reforming infuence of love." The way he said it made the word a mockery.

Rhys ignored it. "And how did you happen to learn of the copper beneath Crickfield?" he asked, still as if only mildly interested.

"Oh, that was a fluke, as I told your Miss Fielding. I came every now and then to see Uncle Edward, just to keep my hand in and keep his resentment against you high. At that point, I didn't want the place, but I thought it might bring in something, and like you, my father has kept me perpetually short of money. And I deserved it far more than you ever did, for I stayed like a dutiful son while you went off to enjoy yourself. A fact you can be sure I never allowed dear Uncle Edward to forget."

He shrugged. "You're fond of talking about your blasted luck, but for once mine seemed to be in. It was sheer luck that I happened to be here once when a mining engineer was tramping through the district. He suggested there might be copper under Crickfield, and it wasn't hard to convince my father to investigate further. Unfortunately, Uncle Edward wasn't as easy. You'd think he would have leapt at the chance to be able to support that damned mausoleum of his, but he wouldn't hear of it, even after the miner's report came through. Can you believe it? He was actually prepared to sit on a fortune of copper in order to keep the great name of Fitzwarren unsullied by an connections to trade. Trade! It would have been laughable if it hadn't been so criminally shortsighted."

He seemed to be enjoying his recital. "I knew he had remade his will by then—with a good deal of persuasion from me, I might add—and so in theory all I had to do was sit and wait. But unfortunately my debts were beginning to pile up, and I couldn't afford to wait. And it was surprisingly easy. He was genuinely ill, though his doctor said he might have gone on for years, and I hadn't years to spare. A slight increase one night in the laudanum he liked to take to help him sleep, and it was all over. And as I suspected, no one even asked any questions."

He smiled, as if enjoying a private jest. "Then I'm afraid my luck began to run out. You always did have all the luck in the family, Rhys. It was unfortunate I couldn't convince my uncle to leave the place to me, though you can be sure I tried. And then my father, if you can believe it, began to show signs of his brother's obsession, and balked at the idea of becoming involved in anything so vulgar as the mining of copper. And even worse, I received word from that fool of a lawyer that you had showed up unexpectedly. It looked like everything was coming apart in my hands."

Again he shrugged. "I thought I had you taken care of, and had even told the fools to bring me that damn talisman ring of yours to prove they'd gotten the right man. It serves me right for not taking care of it myself. They bungled it completely, and then *she* stumbled in. But you always did have the devil's own luck.

"Even so, I thought I was still safe enough, for according to old Kettlewell, you suspected nothing. I thought I would have enough time to track you down and finish the job. But again I reckoned without Miss Fielding."

Alessia froze. "You knew . . . ?"

"Oh, not at first. My father thought you simply

a slightly boring nuisance, but when I heard of your visit I thought it was odd enough to investigate. I still don't know how you managed to guess—"

"I broke into the safe in the library and found the letter from Mr. Maltby," she interrupted calmly.

He looked astonished, and then began to laugh. "The devil you did! I'm beginning to think there's more of your mother in you than I'd thought. Rhys always did have all the luck."

He still looked amused. "It's just run out, however. I tried to be rid of both of you once before, but again you managed to escape. But I promise you I don't intend to fail this time."

"Leave her out of this," Rhys said sharply. "You don't need her."

"How touching! But your little lightskirt is essential to my plans. You played right into my hands there, too, for I understand the connection between you is something of a local scandal. Miss Fielding's relations seem to understand her very well, and have expected for years that she would one day reveal her true colors. I regret that tomorrow you will both be found dead, at the bottom of a ravine. It will seem as if you were eloping, and missed the road in the dark."

"What's the point, if your father won't agree to develop the copper?" demanded Rhys.

"Ah, I can see you still make the mistake of underestimating me. You always did, you know. I was quiet Cousin Owen, reserved and sensible, while you attracted all the attention. I fear if my father continues to be . . . recalcitrant, he will himself die quietly in his sleep one night soon. The shock of losing his brother, you understand, and then you, and the pressures of dealing with his new inheritance. It will all be very sad, but no one will think to question it."

"You're mad!" whispered Alessia involuntarily.

His attention shifted to her. "Perhaps. But I can almost regret there won't be time to plumb your unexpected depths, my dear. You look so angelic, and yet those innocent looks must be deceiving. It is an intriguing combination, but then, my cousin always had excellent taste in high fliers. And if your mother's example is anything to go by, you must—"

He didn't finish, for without warning Rhys had pushed Alessia to the ground, out of harm's way, and launched himself at his cousin.

She lay where she'd fallen, shaken, and watched the struggle that unfolded between them with horrified eyes. She knew that Rhys must still retain some weakness from his recent injuries, and Owen was both whole and desperate. Rhys had managed to grip his cousin's right arm with both of his, and was endeavoring to wrench the pistol away, but she feared at any moment to hear it discharge and see him fall in a heap.

Owen, she saw in horror, had managed to get the pistol around and was trying to aim it at Rhys, but Rhys, with equal determination, was forcing his hand up, preventing him from getting a clear shot.

Then, even as she watched, Rhys's intention became clear to her. He was gradually bending his cousin's arm around, the effort bringing beads of sweat to his brow and the deadly purpose of his face making him look, for the moment, almost a stranger to her.

His cousin, too, must have finally sensed his intent, for at the last minute he tried to release his grip on the pistol. Rhys's hand covered his on the weapon and slowly, inch by inch, forced the pistol round and his cousin's finger back on the trigger. Alessia closed her eyes as Owen seemed to realize, too late, that once more he had lost to his luckier cousin.

The explosion the pistol made in the little clearing deafened her. Alessia lay still for a moment longer, her eyes tightly closed in cowardice; then at last she made herself open them. Owen lay pitched forward on his face in the grass and Rhys was bent double beside him, as if he were going to be sick.

She forced her own nerves to steady then and took charge immediately. She pulled him away and held him until his trembling stopped and the great breaths of air he was dragging into his lungs at last stilled. Then she said quietly, "You had no choice. I know that."

"No," he said, his face still ashen. "But he was still my cousin and I can't forget that."

"In time you will forget this, and remember only when you were boys. I think he was quite mad, you know. He would have murdered his own father for nothing but the possibility of a fortune in copper. He certainly murdered yours."

He straightened a little more. "Yes. And he would have murdered you without a blink. I doubt I will ever be able to forgive him for that. I'm only sorry you had to see it. Let me take you home before I do anything else. I refuse to involve you in this as well."

"Nonsense," she said calmy. "You are the one who must go. It was known your cousin came to get me. I shall report an attempted robbery on the way. Your cousin will have died trying to defend me. After all, you must admit there is a certain irony in that."

He hesitated, then abruptly took her in his arms. "I admit only that you are one woman in a million, and I want to spend the rest of my life with you," he said. "And I am beginning to think even that will not be long enough."

She returned his embrace with heartfelt fervor, but asked hesitantly, "And your uncle? What do you suppose will happen now?"

"I think that my cousin was right, and he had little knowledge of what was going on. I had begun to suspect so long ago. Once he learns of it, I think he will be glad enough to turn Crickfield over to me."

She pulled slightly away at that and regarded him searchingly. "Are you sure that's what you want? I know you never—"

He silenced her in the most effective way possible. When he at last drew back, she was more than breathless, but was not so easily manipulated as that. "Nor have you said anything of your cousin's revelations about me. If you are in the slightest bit shocked or disgusted, I want to know now, before it's too late. It won't change anything. I've already promised to follow you anywhere—even to the ends of the earth if necessary. But I have lived too long with even kindhearted people's mingled horror and pity to want that from you."

For answer he kissed her again, even more roughly. "And I want to hear no more such nonsense from you. As for following me anywhere, I am glad to hear it, for I have been longing to take you on my travels and show you the world. But except that we shall certainly go to Italy for our bride-trip, to reacquaint you with the land of your mother's birth, I fear we will be too busy here for some time to travel. And then, of course, the chances are that you will be too occupied with the children for any extended journeys. But with any luck, by the time they are all in school we can take some time for ourselves. And as my cousin pointed out, I have always been very lucky."

She smiled mistily, but when he would have kissed her again, held him away to look questioningly into his eyes. "Are you *sure*? she asked again.

He pulled off his talisman ring and slipped it on her finger, then closed her hand around it. "You are the only luck I shall need from now on, and the only adventure. If you haven't realized that by now, Angel, I shall be happy to spend the rest of my life trying to prove it to you."

At last she relaxed her hold and let him begin trying.